X

BKM

Fecha

D0928206

Navy Blues

Navy Blues

Debbie Macomber

WHEELER
CHIVERS

This Large Print edition is published by Wheeler Publishing, Waterville, Maine USA and by BBC Audiobooks, Ltd, Bath, England.

Published in 2003 in the U.S. by arrangement with Harlequin Books, S.A.

Published in 2003 in the U.K. by arrangement with Harlequin Enterprises II BV.

U.S. Hardcover 1-58724-509-4   (Romance)
U.K. Hardcover 0-7540-7722-5   (Chivers Large Print)
U.K. Softcover 0-7540-7723-3   (Camden Large Print)

The text of this Large Print edition is unabridged. Other aspects of the book may vary from the original edition.

Set in 16 pt. Plantin by Myrna S. Raven.

Printed in the United States on permanent paper.

British Library Cataloguing-in-Publication Data available

Library of Congress Cataloging-in-Publication Data

Macomber, Debbie.
    Navy blues / Debbie Macomber.
        p.   cm.
    ISBN 1-58724-509-4 (lg. print : hc : alk. paper)
    1. Divorced people — Fiction.   2. Childlessness — Fiction.
3. Large type books.   I. Title.
PS3563.A2364N37 2003

2003058050

Dedicated to
Mary Magdalena Lanz,
July 2, 1909 to May 1, 1988
Beloved Aunt

Special thanks to:
Rose Marie Harris,
wife of MMCM Ralph Harris,
retired U.S. Navy;
Debbie Korrell,
wife of Chief Steven Korrell, USS *Alaska*;
Jane McMahon, RN

Chapter One

Seducing her ex-husband wasn't going to be easy, Carol Kyle decided, but she was determined. More than determined — resolute! Her mind was set, and no one knew better than Steve Kyle how stubborn she could be when she wanted something.

And Carol wanted a baby.

Naturally she had no intention of letting him in on her plans. What he didn't know wouldn't hurt him. Their marriage had lasted five good years, and six bad months. To Carol's way of thinking, which she admitted was a bit twisted at the moment, Steve owed her at least one pregnancy.

Turning thirty had convinced Carol that drastic measures were necessary. Her hormones were jumping up and down, screaming for a chance at motherhood. Her biological clock was ticking away, and Carol swore she could hear every beat of that blasted timepiece. Everywhere she turned, it seemed she was confronted with pregnant women, who served to remind her that her time was running out. If she picked up a magazine, there would be an article on some aspect of parenting. Even her favorite characters on television sitcoms were pregnant. When she found herself wandering through the infant section of her favorite department store, Carol realized drastic measures needed to be taken.

Making the initial contact with Steve hadn't been easy, but she recognized that the first move had to come from her. Getting in touch with her ex-husband after more than a year of complete silence had required two weeks of nerve building. But she'd managed to swallow her considerable pride and do it. Having a woman answer his phone had thrown her for a loop, and Carol had visualized her plans swirling down the drain until she realized the woman was Steve's sister, Lindy.

Her former sister-in-law had sounded pleased to hear from her, and then Lindy had said something that had sent Carol's spirits soaring to the ceiling: Lindy had claimed that Steve missed her dreadfully. Lordy, she hoped that was true. If so, it probably meant he wasn't dating yet. There could be complications if Steve was involved with another woman. On the other hand, there could also be problems if he wasn't involved.

Carol only needed him for one tempestuous night, and then, if everything went according to schedule, Steve Kyle could fade out of her life once more. If she failed to get pregnant . . . well, she'd leap that hurdle when she came to it.

Carol had left a message for Steve a week earlier, and he hadn't returned her call. She wasn't overly concerned. She knew her ex-husband well; he would mull it over carefully before he'd get back to her. He would want her to stew a while first. She'd carefully figured the time element into her schedule of events.

Her dinner was boiling on the stove, and Carol turned down the burner after checking the sweet potatoes with a cooking fork. Glaring at the orange-colored root, she heaved a huge sigh and squelched her growing dislike for the vegetable. After she became pregnant, she swore she would never eat another sweet potato for as long as she lived. A recent news report stated that the starchy vegetable helped increase the level of estrogen in a woman's body. Armed with that information, Carol had been eating sweet potatoes every day for the last two weeks. There had to be enough of the hormone floating around in her body by now to produce triplets.

Noting the potatoes were soft, she drained the water and dumped the steaming roots into her blender. A smile crowded the edges of her mouth. Eating sweet potatoes was a small price to pay for a beautiful baby . . . for Steve's baby.

"Have you called Carol back yet?" Lindy Callaghan demanded of her brother as she walked into the small kitchen of the two-bedroom apartment she shared with her husband and Steve.

Steve Kyle ignored her until she pulled out

9

the chair and plopped down across the table from him. "No," he admitted flatly. He could see no reason to hurry. He already knew what Carol was going to tell him. He'd known it from the minute they'd walked out of the King County Courthouse, the divorce papers clenched in her hot little hands. She was re-marrying. Well, more power to her, but he wasn't going to sit back and blithely let her rub his nose in the fact.

"Steve," Lindy insisted, her face tight with impatience. "It could be something important."

"You told me it wasn't."

"Sure, that's what Carol said, but . . . oh, I don't know, I have the feeling that it really must be. It isn't going to do any harm to call her back."

Methodically Steve turned the page of the evening newspaper and carefully creased the edge before folding it in half and setting it aside. Lindy and Rush, her husband, couldn't be expected to understand his reluctance to phone his ex-wife. He hadn't told either of them the details that had led to his and Carol's divorce. He preferred to keep all thoughts of the disastrous relationship out of his mind. There were plenty of things he could have for-given, but not what Carol had done — not infi-delity.

As a Lieutenant Commander aboard the sub-marine USS *Atlantis*, Steve was at sea for as long as six months out of a year. From the first

10

Carol hadn't seemed to mind sending him off on a three-to-four month cruise. She even used to joke about it, telling him all the projects she planned to complete when he was at sea, and how pleased she was that he would be out of her hair for a while. When he'd returned she'd always seemed happy that he was home, but not exuberant. If anything had gone wrong in his absence — a broken water pipe, car repairs, anything — she'd seen to it herself with barely more than a casual mention.

Steve had been so much in love with her that the little things hadn't added up until later — much later. He'd deceived himself by over-looking the obvious. The physical craving they had for each other had diluted his doubts. Making love with Carol had been so hot it was like a nuclear meltdown. Toward the end she'd been eager for him, but not quite as enthusiastic as in the past. He'd been trusting, blind and incredibly stupid when it came to his ex-wife.

Then by accident he'd learned why she'd become so blasé about his comings and goings. When he left their bed, his loveless, faithless wife had a built-in replacement — her employer, Todd Larson.

It was just short of amazing that Steve hadn't figured it out earlier, and yet when he thought about it, he could almost calculate to the day when she'd started her little affair.

"Steve?"

Lindy's voice cut into his musings, and he lifted his gaze to meet hers. Her eyes were round and dark with concern. Steve experienced a small twinge of guilt for the way he'd reacted to his sister and Rush's marriage. When he'd learned his best friend had married his only sister after a dating period of a mere two weeks, Steve had been furious. He'd made no bones about telling them both the way he felt about their hurry-up wedding. Now he realized his own bitter experience had tainted his reasoning, and he'd long since apologized. It was obvious they were crazy about each other, and Steve had allowed his own misery to bleed into his reaction to their news.

"Okay, okay. I'll return Carol's call," he answered in an effort to appease his younger sibling. He understood all too well how much Lindy wanted him to settle matters with Carol. Lindy was happy, truly happy, and it dismayed her that his life should be at such loose ends.

"When?"

"Soon," Steve promised.

The front door opened, and Rush let himself into the apartment; his arms were loaded with Christmas packages. He paused just inside the kitchen and exchanged a sensual look with his wife. Steve watched the heated gaze and it was like throwing burning acid on his half-healed wounds. He waited a moment for the pain to lessen.

"How'd the shopping go?" Lindy asked, her

silky smooth voice eager and filled with pleasure at the sight of her husband.

"Good," Rush answered and faked a yawn,
"but I'm afraid it wore me out."

Steve playfully rolled his eyes toward the
ceiling and stood, preparing to leave the apartment. "Don't tell me you two are going to take
another nap!"

Lindy's cheeks filled with crimson color and
she looked away. In the past few days the two of
them had taken more naps than a newborn
babe. Even Rush looked a bit chagrined.

"All right, you two," Steve said good-
naturedly, reaching for his leather jacket. "I'll
give you some privacy."

One glance from Lindy told him she was
grateful. Rush stopped Steve on his way out the
door and his eyes revealed his appreciation.
"We've decided to look for a place of our own
right away, but it doesn't look like we'll be able
to move until after the first of the year." He
paused and lowered his gaze, looking almost
embarrassed. "I know this is an inconvenience
for you to keep leaving, but . . ."

"Don't worry about it," Steve countered with
a light chuckle. He patted his friend on the
back. "I was a newlywed once myself."

Steve tried to sound casual about the whole
matter, but doubted if he'd succeeded. Being
constantly exposed to the strong current of love
flowing between his friend and his sister was
damn difficult, because he understood their

need for each other all too well. There'd been a time when a mere look was all that was required to spark flames between him and Carol. Their desire seemed to catch fire and leap to brilliance with a single touch, and they couldn't get to bed fast enough. Steve had been crazy in love with her. Carol had appealed to all his senses and he'd ached with the desire to possess her completely. The only time he felt he'd accomplished that was when he was making love to her. Then and only then was Carol utterly his. And those times were all too brief.

Outside the apartment, the sky was dark with thick gray clouds. Steve walked across the street and headed toward the department stores. He didn't have much Christmas shopping to do, but now appeared to be as good a time for the task as any.

He hesitated in front of a pay phone and released a long, slow breath. He might as well call Carol and be done with it. She wanted to gloat, and he would let her. After all, it was the season to be charitable.

The phone rang just as Carol was coming in the front door. She stopped, set her purse on the kitchen counter and glared at the telephone. Her heart rammed against her rib cage with such force that she had to stop and gather her thoughts. It was Steve. The phone might as well have been spelling out his name in Morse code, she was that sure.

14

"Hello?" she answered brightly, on the third ring.

"Lindy said you phoned." His words were low, flat and emotionless.

"Yes, I did," she murmured, her nerves clamoring.

"Do you want to tell me why, or are you going to make me guess? Trust me, Carol, I'm in no mood to play twenty questions with you."

Oh Lord, this wasn't going to be easy. Steve sounded so cold and uncaring. She'd anticipated it, but it didn't lessen the effect his tone had on her. "I . . . I thought we could talk."

A short, heavy silence followed.

"I'm listening."

"I'd rather we didn't do it over the phone, Steve," she said softly, but not because she'd planned to make her voice silky and smooth. Her vocal chords had tightened and it just came out sounding that way. Her nerves were stretched to their limit, and her heart was pounding in her ear like a charging locomotive.

"Okay," he answered, reluctance evident in every syllable.

"When?" Her gaze scanned the calendar — the timing of this entire venture was of primary importance.

"Tomorrow," he suggested.

Carol's eyes drifted shut as the relief worked its way through her stiff limbs. Her biggest concern was that he would suggest after the Christmas holidays, and then it would be too

15

late and she would have to reschedule everything for January.

"That would be fine," Carol managed. "Would you mind coming to the house?" The two bedroom brick rambler had been awarded to her as part of the divorce settlement.

Again she could feel his hesitation. "As a matter of fact, I would."

"All right," she answered, quickly gathering her wits. His not wanting to come to the house shouldn't have surprised her. "How about coffee at Denny's tomorrow evening?"

"Seven?"

Carol swallowed before answering. "Fine. I'll see you then."

Her hand was still trembling a moment later when she replaced the telephone receiver in its cradle. All along she'd accepted that Steve wasn't going to fall into her bed without some subtle prompting, but from the brusque, impatient sound of his voice, the whole escapade could well be impossible . . . this month. That bothered her. The one pivotal point in her plan was that everything come together quickly. One blazing night of passion could easily be dismissed and forgotten. But if she were to continue to invite him back one night a month, several months running, then he just might catch on to what she was doing.

Still, when it had come to interpreting her actions in the past, Steve had shown a shocking lack of insight. Thankfully their troubles had never intruded in the bedroom. Their marriage relationship had been a jumbled mess of doubts and misunderstandings, accusations and regrets, but their love life had always been vigorous and lusty right up until the divorce, astonishing as it seemed now.

At precisely seven the following evening, Carol walked into Denny's Restaurant on Seattle's Capitol Hill. The first year she and Steve had been married, they'd had dinner there once a month. Money had been tight because they'd been saving for a down payment on the house, and an evening out, even if it was only Saturday night at Denny's, had been a real treat.

Two steps into the restaurant Carol spotted her former husband sitting in a booth by the window. She paused and experienced such a wealth of emotion that advancing even one step more would have been impossible. Steve had no right to look this good — far better than she remembered. In the thirteen months since she'd last seen him, he'd changed considerably. Matured. His features were sharper, clearer, more intense. His lean good looks were all the more prominent, his handsome masculine features vigorous and tanned even in December. A few strands of gray hair streaked his temple, adding a distinguished air.

His gaze caught hers and Carol sucked in a deep, calming breath, her steps nearly faltering as she advanced toward him. His eyes had changed the most, she decided. Where once they had been warm and caressing, now they were cool and calculating. They narrowed on her, his mistrust shining through as bright as any beacon.

Carol experienced a moment of panic as his gaze seemed to strip away the last shreds of her pride. It took all her willpower to force a smile to her lips.

"Thank you for coming," she said, and slipped into the red upholstered seat across from him.

The waitress came with a glass coffeepot, and Carol turned over her cup, which the woman promptly filled after placing menus on the table.

"It feels cold enough to snow," Carol said as a means of starting conversation. It was eerie that she could have been married to Steve all those years and feel as if he were little more than a stranger. He gave her that impression now. This hard, impassive man was one she didn't know nearly as well as the one who had once been her lover, her friend and her husband.

"You're looking fit," Steve said after a moment, a spark of admiration glinting in his gaze.

"Thank you." A weak smile hovered over her lips. "You, too. How's the Navy treating you?"

"Good."

"Are you still on the *Atlantis*?"

He nodded shortly.

Silence.

Carol groped for something more to say. "It was a surprise to discover that Lindy's living in Seattle."

"Did she tell you she married Rush?"

Carol noted the way his brows drew together and darkened his face momentarily when he mentioned the fact. "I didn't realize Lindy even knew Rush," Carol said, and took a sip of the coffee.

"They were married two weeks after they met. Lord, I can't believe it yet."

"Two weeks? That doesn't sound anything like Rush. I remember him as being so methodical about everything."

Steve's frown relaxed, but only a little. "Apparently they fell in love."

Carol knew Steve well enough to recognize the hint of sarcasm in his voice, as if he were telling her what a mockery that emotion was. In their instance it had certainly been wasted. Sadly wasted.

"Are they happy?" That was the important thing as far as Carol was concerned.

"They went through a rough period a while back, but since the *Mitchell* docked they seem to have mended their fences."

Carol dropped her gaze to her cup as reality cut sharply into her heart. "That's more than we did."

"As you recall," he said harshly, under his breath, "there wasn't any fence left to repair. The night you started sleeping with Todd

Larson, you destroyed our marriage."

Carol didn't rise to the challenge, although Steve had all but slapped her face with it. There was nothing she could say to exonerate herself, and she'd given up explaining the facts to him more than a year ago. Steve chose to believe what he wanted. She'd tried, God knew, to set the record straight. Todd had been her employer and her friend, but never anything more. Carol had pleaded with Steve until she was blue with exasperation, but it hadn't done her any good. Rehashing the same argument now wasn't going to help either of them.

Silence stretched between them and was broken by the waitress who had returned to their booth, pad and pen in hand. "Have you decided?"

Carol hadn't even glanced at the menu. "Do you have sweet-potato pie?"

"No, but pecan is the special this month."

Carol shook her head, ignoring the strange look Steve was giving her. "Just coffee then."

"Same here," Steve added.

The woman replenished both their cups and left.

"So how is good ol' Todd?"

His question lacked any real interest, and Carol had already decided her former boss was a subject they'd best avoid. "Fine," she lied. She had no idea how Todd was doing, since she hadn't worked for Larson Sporting Goods for over a year. She'd been offered a better job with

Boeing and had been employed at the airplane company since before the divorce was final.

"I'm glad to hear it," Steve said with a soft snicker. "I suppose you called this little meeting to tell me the two of you are finally going to be married."

"No. Steve, please, I didn't call to talk about Todd."

He arched his brows in mock consternation. "I'm surprised. What's the matter, is wife number one still giving him problems? You mean to tell me their divorce hasn't gone through?"

A shattering feeling of hopelessness nearly choked Carol, and she struggled to meet his gaze without flinching. Steve was still so bitter, so intent on making her suffer.

"I really would prefer it if we didn't discuss Todd or Joyce."

"Fine. What do you want to talk about?" He checked his watch as if to announce he had plenty of other things he could be doing and didn't want to waste precious time with her.

Carol had carefully planned everything she was going to say. Each sentence had been rehearsed several times over in her mind, and now it seemed so trite and ridiculous, she couldn't manage a single word.

"Well?" he demanded. "Since you don't want to rub my nose in the fact that you're marrying Todd, what could you possibly have to tell me?"

Carol gestured with her hand, her fingers trembling. "It's Christmastime," she murmured.

"Congratulations, you've glanced at a calendar lately." He looked straight through her with eyes as hard as diamond bits.

"I thought . . . well, you know, that we could put our differences aside for a little while and at least be civil to each other."

His eyes narrowed. "What possible reason could there be for us to have anything to do with each other? You mean nothing to me, and I'm sure the feeling is mutual."

"You were my husband for five years."

"So?"

She rearranged the silverware several times, choosing not to look at Steve. He wore his anger like a tight pair of shoes and sitting across from him was almost too painful to bear.

"We loved each other once," she said after a drawn-out, strained moment.

"I loved my dog once, too," he came back. One corner of his mouth was pulled down, and his eyes had thinned to narrow slits. "What does having cared about each other have to do with anything now?"

Carol couldn't answer his question. She knew the divorce had made him bitter, but she'd counted on this long time apart to have healed some of his animosity.

"What did you do for the holidays last year?" she asked, refusing to argue with him. She wasn't going to allow him to rile her into losing her temper. He'd played that trick once too often, and she was wise to his game.

"What the hell difference does it make to you how I spent Christmas?"

This wasn't going well, Carol decided — not the least bit as she'd planned. Steve seemed to think she wanted him to admit he'd been miserable without her.

"I . . . I spent the day alone," she told him softly, reluctantly. Their divorce had been final three weeks before the holiday and Carol's emotions had been so raw she'd hardly been able to deal with the usual festivities connected with the holiday.

"I wasn't alone," Steve answered with a cocky half smile that suggested that whoever he was with had been pleasant company, and he hadn't missed her in the least.

Carol didn't know how anyone could look so damned insolent and sensuous at the same moment. It required effort to keep her chin up and meet his gaze, but she managed.

"So *you* were alone," he added. The news appeared to delight him. "That's what happens when you mess around with a married man, my dear. In case you haven't figured it out yet, Todd's wife and family will always come first. That's the other woman's sad lot in life."

Carol went still all over. She felt as though her entire body had turned to stone. She didn't breathe, didn't move, didn't so much as blink.

23

The pain spread out in waves, circling first her throat and then her chest, working its way down to her abdomen, cinching her stomach so tightly that she thought she might be sick. The whole room seemed to fade away and the only thing she was sure about was that she had to get out of the restaurant. Fast.

Her fingers fumbled with the snap of her purse as she opened her wallet. Her hands weren't any more steady as she placed several coins by the coffee cup and scooted out of her seat.

Mutely Steve watched Carol walk out of the restaurant and called himself every foul name that he could come up with from his extensive Navy vocabulary. He hadn't meant to say those things. Hadn't intended to lash out at her. But he hadn't been able to stop himself.

He'd lied, too, in an effort to salvage his pride. Lied rather than give her the satisfaction of knowing he'd spent last Christmas Day miserable and alone. It had been the worst holiday of his life. The pain of the divorce had still ached like a lanced boil, while everyone around him had been celebrating and exchanging gifts, their happiness like a ball and chain shackling his heart. This year didn't hold much prospect for happiness, either. Lindy and Rush would prefer to spend the day alone, although they'd gone out of their way to convince him otherwise. But Steve wasn't stupid and had already made other plans. He'd volunteered for watch Christmas Day so that a fellow officer could spend time with his family.

Gathering his thoughts about Carol, Steve experienced a healthy dose of regret about the way he'd behaved toward his ex-wife.

She'd looked good, he admitted reluctantly — better than he'd wanted her to look for his own peace of mind. From the moment they'd met, he'd felt the vibrant energy that radiated from her. Thirteen months apart hadn't diminished that. He'd known the minute she walked into Denny's; he'd felt her presence the instant the door opened. She wore her thick blond hair shorter than he remembered so that it fell forward and hugged the sides of her face, the ends curling under slightly, giving her a Dutch-boy look. As always, her metallic blue eyes were magnetic, irrevocably drawing his gaze. She looked small and fragile, and the desire to protect and love her had come at him with all the force of a wrecking ball slamming against his chest. He knew differently, but it hadn't seemed to change the way he felt — Carol needed him about as much as the Navy needed more salt water.

Sliding out of the booth, Steve laid a bill on the table and left. Outside, the north wind sent a chill racing up his arms and he buried his hands into his pants pockets as he headed toward the parking lot.

Surprise halted his progress when he spied

Carol leaning against the fender of her car. Her shoulders were slumped, her head hanging as though she were burdened by a terrible weight.

Once more Steve was swamped with regret. He had never learned the reason she'd phoned. He started walking toward her, not knowing what he intended to say or do.

She didn't glance up when he joined her.

"You never said why you phoned," he said in a wounded voice after a moment of silence.

"It isn't important . . . I told Lindy that."

"If it wasn't to let me know you're remarrying, then it's because you want something."

She looked up and tried to smile, and the feeble effort cut straight through Steve's resolve to forget he'd ever known or loved her. It was useless to try.

"I don't think it'll work," Carol said sadly.

"What?"

She shook her head.

"If you need something, just ask!" he shouted, using his anger as a defense mechanism. Carol had seldom wanted anything from him. It must be important for her to contact him now, especially after their divorce.

"Christmas Day," she whispered brokenly. "I don't want to spend it alone."

Chapter Two

Until Carol spoke, she hadn't known how much she wanted Steve to spend Christmas Day with her — and not for the reasons she'd been plotting. She sincerely missed Steve. He'd been both lover and friend, and now he was neither; the sense of loss was nearly overwhelming.

He continued to stare at her, and regret worked its way across his features. The success of her plan hinged on his response and she waited, almost afraid to breathe, for his answer.

"Carol, listen . . ." He paused and ran his hand along the back of his neck, his brow puckered with a condensed frown.

Carol knew him well enough to realize he was carefully composing his thoughts. She was also aware that he was going to refuse her! She knew it as clearly as if he'd spoken the words aloud. She swallowed the hurt, although she couldn't keep her eyes from widening with pain. When Steve had presented her with the divorce papers, Carol had promised herself she would never give him the power to hurt her again. Yet here she was, handing him the knife and exposing her soul.

She could feel her heart thumping wildly in her chest and fought to control the emotions that swamped her. "Is it so much to ask?" she whispered, and the words fell broken from her lips.

"I've got the watch."

"On Christmas . . ." She hadn't expected that, hadn't figured it into the scheme of things. In other words, the excuse of Christmas wasn't going to work. Ultimately her strategy would fail, and she would end up spending the holiday alone.

"I'd do it if I could," Steve told her in a straightforward manner that convinced her he was telling the truth. She felt somewhat less disappointed.

"Thank you for that," she said, and reached out to touch his hand, in a small gesture of appreciation. Amazingly he didn't draw away from her, which gave her renewed hope.

A reluctant silence stretched between them. There'd been a time when they couldn't say enough to each other, and now there was nothing.

"I suppose I'd better get back." Steve spoke first.

"Me, too," she answered brightly, perhaps a little too brightly. "It was good to see you again . . . you're looking well."

"You, too." He took a couple of steps backward, but still hadn't turned away. Swallowing down her disappointment, Carol retrieved the car keys from the bottom of her purse and turned to climb into her Honda. It dawned on her then, hit her square between the eyes. If not Christmas Day then . . .

"Steve," she whirled back around, her eyes flashing.

"Carol." He called her name at the same moment.

They laughed and the sound fell rusty and awkward between them.

"You first," he said, and gestured toward her. The corner of his mouth was curved upward in a half smile.

"What about Christmas Eve?"

He nodded. "I was just thinking the same thing."

Carol felt the excitement bubble up inside her like fizz in a club soda. A grin broke out across her face as she realized nothing had been lost and everything was yet to be gained. Somewhere in the distance, Carol was sure she could hear the soft, lilting strains of a Brahms lullaby. "Could you come early enough for dinner?"

Again, he nodded. "Six?"

"Perfect. I'll look forward to it."

"I will, too."

He turned and walked away from her then, and it was all Carol could do to keep from doing a war dance, jumping up and down around the car. Instead she rubbed her bare hands together as though the friction would ease some of the excitement she was feeling. Steve hadn't a clue how memorable this one night would be. Not a clue!

"Your mood has certainly improved lately," Lindy commented as Steve walked into the kitchen whistling a lively Christmas carol.

His sister's words stopped him. "My mood has?"

"You've been downright chipper all week."

He shrugged his shoulders, hoping the action would discount his cheerful attitude. " 'Tis the season."

"I don't suppose your meeting with Carol has anything to do with it?"

His sister eyed him skeptically, seeking his confidence, but Steve wasn't going to give it. This dinner with his ex-wife was simply the meeting of two lonely people struggling to make it through the holidays. Nothing less and certainly nothing more. Although he'd been looking for Carol to deny that she was involved with Todd, she hadn't. Steve considered her refusal to talk about the other man as good as an admission of guilt. That bastard had left her alone for Christmas two years running.

If Lindy was right and his mood had improved, Steve decided, it was simply because he was going to be out of his sister and Rush's hair for the evening; the newlyweds could spend their first Christmas Eve together without a third party butting in.

Steve reached for his coat, and Lindy turned around, her dark eyes wide with surprise. "You're leaving."

Steve nodded, buttoning the thick wool jacket.

"But . . . it's Christmas Eve."

"I know." He tucked the box of candy under his arm and lifted the bright red poinsettia he'd purchased on impulse earlier in the day.

"Where are you going?"

Steve would have liked to say a friend's house, but that wouldn't be true. He didn't know how to classify his relationship with Carol. Not a friend. Not a lover. More than an acquaintance, less than a wife.

"You're going to Carol's, aren't you?" Lindy prompted.

The last thing Steve wanted was his sister to get the wrong impression about this evening with Carol, because that's all there was going to be. "It's not what you think."

Lindy raised her hands in mock consternation. "I'm not thinking a single thing, except that it's good to see you smile again."

Steve's frown was heavy with purpose. "Well, don't read more into it than there is."

"Are the two of you going to talk?" Lindy asked, and her dark eyes fairly danced with deviltry.

"We're going to eat, not talk," Steve explained with limited patience. "We don't have anything in common anymore. I'll probably be home before ten."

"Whatever you say, " Lindy answered, but her lips twitched with the effort to suppress a knowing smile. "Have a good time."

Steve chose not to answer that comment and left the apartment, but as soon as he was outside, he discovered he was whistling again and stopped abruptly.

Carol slipped the compact disk into the player and set the volume knob so that the soft Christmas music swirled festively through the house. A small turkey was roasting in the oven, stuffed with Steve's favorite sage dressing. Two pies were cooling on the kitchen counter — pumpkin for Steve, mincemeat for her. To be on the safe side a sweet-potato-pecan pie was in the fridge.

Carol chose a red silk dress that whispered enticingly against her soft skin. Her makeup and perfume had been applied with a subtle hand. Everything was ready.

Well, almost everything.

She and Steve were two different people now, and there was no getting around the fact. Regretting the past was an exercise in futility, and yet Carol had been overwhelmed these past few days with the realization that the divorce had been wrong. Very wrong. All the emotion she'd managed to bury this past year had seeped to the surface since her meeting with Steve and she couldn't remember a time when she'd been more confused.

She wanted a child, and she was using her ex-husband. More than once in the past week, she'd been forced to deal with twinges of guilt. But there was no going back. It would be impossible to recapture what had been between them before the divorce. There could be no reconciliation. Even more difficult than the past, Carol had trouble dealing with the present. They couldn't come in contact with each other without the sparks igniting. It made everything more difficult. They were both too stubborn, too temperamental, too obstinate.

And it was ruining their lives.

Carol felt they couldn't go back and yet they couldn't step forward, either. The idea of seducing Steve and getting pregnant had, in the beginning, been entirely selfish. She wanted a baby and she considered Steve the best candidate . . . the only candidate. After their one short meeting at the restaurant, Carol knew her choice of the baby's father went far beyond the practical. A part of her continued to love Steve, and probably always would. She wanted his child because it was the only part of him she would ever be able to have.

Everything hinged on the outcome of this dinner. Carol pressed her hands over her flat stomach and issued a fervent prayer that she was fertile. Twice in the past hour she'd taken her temperature, praying her body would do its part in this master plan. Her temperature was slightly elevated, but that could be caused by the hot sensation that went through her at the thought of sharing a bed with Steve again. Or it could be sheer nerves.

All day she'd been feeling anxious and rest-less with anticipation. She was convinced Steve would take one look at her and instantly know she intended for him to spend the night. The crux of her scheme was for Steve to think their making love was *his* idea. Again and again, her plans for the evening circled her mind, slowly, like the churning blades of a windmill stirring the air.

The doorbell chimed, and inhaling a calming breath, Carol forced a smile, walked across the room and opened the door for her ex-husband. "Merry Christmas," she said softly.

Steve handed her the poinsettia as though he couldn't get rid of the flower fast enough. His gaze didn't quite meet hers. In fact, he seemed to be avoiding looking at her, which pleased Carol because it told her that the red dress was having exactly the effect she'd hoped for.

"Thank you for the flower," she said and set it in the middle of the coffee table. "You didn't need to do that."

"I remembered how you used to buy three and four of those silly things each year and fig-ured one more couldn't hurt."

"It was thoughtful of you, and I appreciate it." She held out her hand to take his coat.

Steve placed a small package under the tree and gave her a shy look. "Frangos," he ex-plained awkwardly. "I suppose they're still your favorite candy."

"Yes. I have a little something for you, too."

Steve peeled off his heavy jacket and handed it to her. "I'm not looking for any gifts from you. I brought the flowers and candy because I wanted to contribute something toward dinner."

"My gift isn't much, Steve."

"Save it for someone else. Okay?"

Her temper nearly slipped then, but Carol managed to keep it intact. Her smile was just a little more forced when she turned from hanging his jacket in the hall closet, but she hoped he hadn't noticed.

"Would you like a hot-buttered rum before we eat?" she offered.

"That sounds good."

He followed her into the kitchen and brought the bottle of rum down from the top cupboard while she put water on to boil.

"When did you cut your hair?" he asked unexpectedly.

Absently Carol's fingers touched the straight, thick strands that crowded the side of her head. "Several months ago now."

"I liked it better when you wore it longer."

Gritting her teeth, she managed to bite back the words to inform him that she styled her hair to suit herself these days, not him.

Steve saw the flash of irritation in his ex-wife's eyes and felt a little better. The comment about her hair wasn't what she'd wanted to hear; she'd been waiting for him to tell her how beautiful she looked. The problem was, he hadn't been able to take his eyes off her from the moment he entered the house. The wisecrack was a result of one flirtatious curl of blond hair that swayed when she moved. He hadn't been able to look past that single golden lock. Neither could he stop staring at the shape of her lips nor the curve of her chin, nor the appealing color of her china blue eyes. When he'd met her at Denny's the other night he'd been on the defensive, waiting for her to drop her bombshell. All his protective walls were lowered now. He would have liked to blame it on the Christmas holidays, but he realized it was more than that, and what he saw gave him cause to tremble. Carol was as sensuous and appealing to him as she'd always been. Perhaps more so.

Already he knew what was going to happen. They would spend half the evening verbally circling each other in an anxious search for common ground. But there wasn't one for them . . . not anymore. Tonight was an evening out of sequence, and when it had passed they would return to their respective lives.

When Carol finished mixing their drinks, they wandered into the living room and talked. The alcohol seemed to alleviate some of the tension. Steve filled the silence with details of what had been happening in Lindy's life and in his career.

"You've done well for yourself," Carol admitted, and there was a spark of pride in her eyes that warmed him.

Steve didn't inquire about her career because it would involve asking about Todd, and the man was a subject he'd sworn he would avoid at all costs. Carol didn't volunteer any information, either. She knew the unwritten ground rules.

A half hour later, Steve helped her carry their meal to the table.

"You must have been cooking all day."

She grinned and nodded. "It gave me something to do."

The table was loaded with sliced turkey, creamy potatoes, giblet gravy, stuffing, fresh broccoli, sweet potatoes and fruit salad.

Carol asked him to light the candles and when Steve had, they sat down to eat. Sitting directly across the table from her, Steve found he was mesmerized by her mouth as she ate. With all his might he tried to remember the reasons he'd divorced Carol. Good God, she was captivating — too damn good to look at for his own peace of mind. Her hands moved gracefully, raising the fork from her plate to her mouth in motions as elegant as those of a symphony director. He shouldn't be enjoying watching her this much, and he realized he would pay the price later when he returned to the apartment and the loneliness overtook him once more.

When he'd finished the meal, he leaned against the shield-back dining-room chair and placed his hands over his stomach. "I can't remember when I've had a better dinner."

"There's pie . . ."

"Not now," he countered quickly and shook his head. "I'm too full to down another bite. Maybe later."

"Coffee?"

"Please."

Carol carried their dishes to the sink, stuck the leftovers in the refrigerator, and returned with the glass coffeepot. She filled both their cups, returned it to the kitchen and then took her seat opposite him. She rested her elbows on the table, and smiled.

Despite his best intentions through a good portion of the meal, Steve hadn't been able to keep his eyes away from her. The way she was sitting — leaning forward, her elbows on the tabletop — caused her breasts to push together and more than amply fill the bodice of her dress. His breath faltered someplace between his lungs and his throat at the alluring sight she made. He could have sworn she wasn't wearing a bra. Carol had fantastic breasts and Steve watched, captivated, as their tips beaded against the shiny material. They seemed to be pointing directly at him, issuing a silent invitation that asked him to fondle and taste them. Against his will, his groin began to swell until he was throbbing with painful need. Disconcerted, he dropped his gaze to the steaming cup of coffee. With his hands shaking, he took a sip of his coffee and nearly scalded the tender skin inside his mouth.

"That was an excellent dinner," he repeated, after a moment of silence.

"You're not sorry you came, are you?" she asked unexpectedly, studying him. The intent look that crowded her face demanded all Steve's attention. Her skin was pale and creamy in the muted light, her eyes wide and inquiring, as though the answer to her question was of the utmost importance.

"No," he admitted reluctantly. "I'm glad I'm here."

His answer pleased her and she smiled, looking tender and trusting, and Steve wondered how he could ever have doubted her. He knew what she'd done — knew that she'd purposely destroyed their marriage — and in that moment, it didn't matter. He wanted her again. He wanted to hold her warm and willing body in his arms. He wanted to bury himself so deep inside her that she would never desire another man for as long as they both lived.

"I'll help you with the dishes," he said, and rose so abruptly that he nearly knocked over the chair.

"I'll do them later." She got to her feet as well. "But if you want to do something, I'd appreciate a little help with the tree."

"The tree?" The words sounded as foreign as an obscure language.

"Yes, it's only half decorated. I couldn't reach the tallest limbs. Will you help?"

He shrugged. "Sure." He could have sworn that Carol was relieved, and he couldn't imagine why. The Christmas tree looked fine to him. There were a few bare spots, but nothing too noticeable.

Carol dragged a dining-room chair into the living room and pulled a box of ornaments out from underneath the end table.

"You're knitting?" Steve asked, hiding a smile as his gaze fell on the strands of worsted yarn. Carol had to be the worst knitter in the world, yet she tackled one project after another, seeming oblivious of any lack of talent. There had been a time when he could tease her about it, but he wasn't sure his insight would be appreciated now.

She glanced away as though she feared his comment.

"Don't worry, I'm not going to tease you," he told her, remembering the time she'd proudly presented him with a sweater she'd made herself — the left sleeve had been five inches longer than the right. He'd tried it on and she'd taken one look at him and burst into tears. It was one of the few times he could ever remember Carol crying.

Carol dragged the chair next to the tree and raised her leg to stand on it.

Steve stopped her. "I thought you wanted me to do that?"

"No, I need you to hand me the ornaments and then stand back and tell me how they look."

"Carol . . . if I placed the ornaments on the tree, you wouldn't need the chair."

She looked at him and sighed. "I'd rather do it. You don't mind, do you?"

He didn't know why she was so determined to hang the decorations herself, but it didn't make much difference to him. "No, if you want to risk your fool neck, feel free."

She grinned and raised herself so that she was standing on the padded cushion of the chair. "Okay, hand me one," she said, tossing him a look over her shoulder.

Steve gave her a shiny glass bulb, and he noted how good she smelled. Roses and some other scent he couldn't define wrapped gently around him. Carol stretched out her arms and reached for the tallest branch. Her dress rose a solid five inches and exposed the back of her creamy smooth thighs and a fleeting glimpse of the sweet curve of her buttocks. Steve knotted his hands into fists at his sides to keep from touching her. It would be entirely plausible for him to grip her waist and claim he was frightened she would tumble from her perch. But if he allowed that to happen, his hands would slip and soon he would be cupping that cute rounded bottom. Once he touched her, Steve knew he would never be able to stop. He clenched his teeth and inhaled deeply through his nose. Having Carol standing there, exposing herself in this unconscious way, was more than a mere man could resist. At this point, he was willing to use any excuse to be close to her once more.

Carol lowered her arms, her dress fell back into place and Steve breathed normally again. He thought he was safe from further temptation until she twisted around. Her ripe, full breasts filled the front of her dress, their shape clearly defined against the thin fabric. If he'd been guessing about the bra before, he was now certain. She wasn't wearing one.

"I'm ready for another ornament," she said softly.

Like a blind man, Steve turned and fumbled for a second glass bulb. He handed it to her and did everything within his power to keep his gaze away from her breasts.

"How does that one look?" Carol asked.

"Fine," Steve answered gruffly.

"Steve?"

"Don't you think that's enough decorations, for God's sake?"

His harsh tone was as much a surprise to him as it obviously was to Carol.

"Yes, of course."

She sounded disappointed, but that couldn't be helped. Steve moved to her side once more and offered her his hand to help her down. His foot must have hit against one leg of the chair because it jerked forward. Perhaps it was something she did, Steve wasn't sure, but whatever happened caused the chair to teeter on the thick carpet.

With a small cry of alarm, Carol threw out her arms.

With reflexes born of years of military training, Steve's hands shot out like bullets to catch her. The chair fell sideways onto the floor, but Steve's grip on Carol's waist anchored her firmly against his torso. Their breathing was labored, and Steve sighed with relief that she hadn't fallen. It was on the tip of his tongue to berate her, call her a silly goose for not letting him place the glass bulbs on the tree, chastise her for being such a fool. She shouldn't put herself at risk over something as nonsensical as a Christmas tree. But none of the words made it to his lips.

Their gazes were even, her haunting eyes stared into his and said his name as clearly as if it were spoken. Carol's feet remained several inches off the floor, and still Steve held on to her, unable to release her. His heart was pounding frantically with wonder as he raised a finger and touched her soft throat. His gaze continued to delve into hers. He wanted to set her back on the carpet, to free them both from this invisible grip before it maimed them, but he couldn't seem to find the strength to let her go.

Slowly she slid down his front, between his braced feet, crimping the skirt of her dress between them. Once she was secure, he noted that her lower abdomen was tucked snugly in the joint between his thighs. The throbbing in his groin began again, and he held in a groan that threatened to emanate from deep within his chest.

He longed to kiss her more than he'd ever wanted anything in his life, and only the greatest strength of will kept him from claiming her sweet mouth with his own.

She'd betrayed him once, crippled him with her deceit. Steve had sworn he would never allow her to use him again, yet his arguments burned away like dry timber in a forest fire.

His thumb found her moist lips and brushed back and forth as though the action would be enough to satisfy either of them. It didn't. If anything, it created an agony even more powerful. His heart leaped into a hard, fast rhythm that made him feel breathless and weak. Before he could stop himself, his finger lifted her chin and his mouth glided over hers. Softly. Moistly. Satin against satin.

Carol sighed.

Steve groaned.

She weakened in his arms and closed her eyes. Steve kissed her a second time and thrust his tongue deep into her mouth, his need so strong it threatened to consume him. His hand was drawn to her breast, as if caught by a vise and carried there against his will. He cupped the rounded flesh, and his finger teased the nipple until it beaded and swelled against his palm. Carol whimpered.

He had to touch her breasts again. Had to know for himself their velvet smoothness. Releasing a ragged sigh, he reached behind her and peeled down her zipper. She was as eager as he when he lowered the top of her dress and exposed her naked front.

Her hands were around his neck, and she slanted her mouth over his, rising to her tiptoes as she leaned her weight into his. Steve's mouth quickly abandoned hers to explore the curve of her neck and then lower to the rosy tips of her firm, proud breasts. His moist tongue traced circles around the pebbled nipples until Carol shuddered and plowed her fingers through his hair.

"Steve . . . oh, I've missed you so much." She repeated the sentence over and over again, but the words didn't register in his clouded mind. When they did, he went cold. She may have missed him, may have hungered for his touch, but she hadn't been faithful. The thought crippled him, and he went utterly still.

Carol must have sensed his withdrawal, because she dropped her arms. Her shoulders were heaving as though she'd been running in a heated race. His own breathing wasn't any more regular.

Abruptly Steve released her and stumbled two paces back.

"That shouldn't have happened," he announced in a hoarse whisper.

Carol regarded him with a wounded look but said nothing.

"I've got to get out of here," he said, expelling the words on the tail end of a sigh.

Carol's gaze widened and she shook her head.

"Carol, we aren't married anymore. This shouldn't be happening."

"I know." She lowered her gaze to the carpet.

Steve walked to the hall closet and reached for his jacket. His actions felt as if they were in slow motion — as if every gravitational force in the universe was pulling at him.

He paused, his hand clenching the doorknob. "Thank you for dinner."

Carol nodded, and when he turned back, he saw that her eyes had filled with tears and she was biting her bottom lip to hold them back. One hand held the front of her dress across her bare breasts.

"Carol . . ."

She looked at him with soft, appealing eyes and held out her hand. "Don't go," she begged softly. "Please don't leave me. I need you so much."

Chapter Three

Carol could see the battle raging in Steve's tight features. She swallowed down the tears and refused to release his gaze, which remained locked with her own.

"We're not married anymore," he said in a voice that shook with indecision.

"I . . . don't care." Swallowing her pride, she took one small step toward him. If he wouldn't come to her, then she was going to him. Her knees felt incredibly weak, as though she were walking after being bedridden for a long while.

"Carol . . ."

She didn't stop until she was standing directly in front of him. Then slowly, with infinite care, she released her hold on the front of her dress and allowed it to fall free, baring her breasts. Steve rewarded her immediately with a swift intake of breath, and then it seemed as if he stopped breathing completely. Carol slipped her flattened hands up his chest and leaned her body into his. When she felt his rock-hard arousal pressing against her thigh, she closed her eyes to disguise the triumph that zoomed through her blood like a shot of adrenaline.

Steve held himself stiffly against her, refusing to yield to her softness; his arms hung motionless at his sides. He didn't push her away, but he didn't welcome her into his embrace, either.

Five years of marriage had taught Carol a good deal about her husband's body. She knew what pleasured him most, knew what would drive him to the edge of madness, knew how to make him want her until there was nothing else in their world.

Standing on the tips of her toes, she locked her arms tightly around his neck and raised her soft lips to gently brush her mouth over his. Her kiss was as moist and light as dew on a summer rose. Steve's lashes dropped and she could feel the torment of the battle that raged in his troubled mind.

Slightly elevating one foot, she allowed her shoe to slip off her toes. It fell almost silently to the floor. Carol nearly laughed aloud at the expression that came over Steve's contorted features. He knew what was coming, and against his will, Carol could see that he welcomed it. In a leisurely exercise, she raised her nylon-covered foot and slid it down the backside of his leg. Again and again her thigh and calf glided over his, each caressing stroke moved higher and higher on his leg, bringing her closer to her objective.

When Steve's hand closed, almost painfully, over her thigh, Carol knew she'd won. He held her there for a timeless moment, neither moving nor breathing.

"Kiss me," he ordered, and the words seemed to be ground out from between clenched teeth.

Although Carol had fully intended to comply with his demand, she apparently didn't do it fast enough to suit her ex-husband. He groaned and his free hand locked around the back of her head, compelling her mouth to his. Driven by urgency, his kiss was forceful and demanding, almost grinding, as if he sought to punish her for making him want her so much. Carol allowed him to ravage her mouth, giving him everything he wanted, everything he asked for, until finally she gasped for breath and broke away briefly. Steve brought her mouth back to his, and gradually his kisses softened until Carol thought she was sure her whole body would burst into flames. Sensing this, Steve moved his hand from the back of her head and began to massage her breast in a leisurely circular motion, his palm centering on her nipple. Her whole torso started to pulsate under his gentle touch.

Carol arched her spine to grant him easier access, and tossed back her head as his fingers worked their magic. Then his hand left her breast, and she wanted to protest until she felt his fingers slip around her other thigh and lift her completely off the carpet, raising her so that their mouths were level, their breath mingling, moist and excited.

They paused and gazed into each other's eyes. Steve's were filled with surprise and wonder. Carol met that look and smiled with a rediscovered joy that burst from deep within her. An inner happiness that had vanished from her life the moment Steve had walked away from her, returned. She leaned forward and very gently rubbed her mouth across his, creating a moist, delicious friction. Gently her tongue played over the seam of his lips, sliding back and forth, teasing him, testing him in a love game that had once been familiar between them.

Carol gently caught his lower lip between her teeth and sucked on it, playing with it while darting the tip of her tongue in and out of his mouth.

The effect on Steve was electric. His mouth claimed hers in an urgent kiss that drove the oxygen from her lungs. Then, with a strength that astonished her, he lifted her even higher until his mouth closed over her left breast, rolling his tongue over her nipple, then sucking at it greedily, taking in more and more of her breast.

Carol thought she was going to go crazy with the tidal wave of sensation that flooded her being. She locked her legs around his waist and braced her hands against his shoulders. His mouth and tongue alternated from one breast to the other until she was convinced that if he didn't take her soon, she was going to faint in his arms.

Braced against the closet door, Steve used what leverage he could to inch his hand up the inside of her thigh. His exploring fingers reached higher and higher, then paused when he encountered a nylon barrier. He groaned his frustration.

Carol was so weak with longing that if he didn't carry her voluntarily into the bedroom soon, she was going to demand that he make love to her right there on the entryway floor.

"You weren't wearing a bra," he chastised her in a husky thwarted voice. "I was hoping . . ."

He didn't need to finish for Carol to know what he was talking about. When they were married, she'd often worn a garter belt with her nylons instead of panty hose so their love-making wouldn't be impeded.

"I want you," she whispered, her hands framing his face. "But if you think it would be best to leave . . . go now. The choice is yours."

His gaze locked with hers, Steve marched wordlessly across the living room and down the long hallway to the bedroom that had once been theirs.

"Not here," she told him. "I sleep there now," she explained, pointing to the room across the hall.

Steve switched directions and marched into the smaller bedroom, not stopping until he reached the queen-size bed. For one crazy second, Carol thought he meant to drop her on top of the mattress and storm right out of the house. Instead he continued to hold her, the look in his eyes wild and uncertain.

Carol's eyes met his. She was nearly choking

on the sadness that threatened to overwhelm her. Tentatively she raised one hand and pressed it to the side of his face, her eyes wide, her heart pounding so hard she was sure the sound of it would soon bring down the walls.

To her surprise, Steve tenderly placed her on the bed, braced one knee against the edge of the mattress and leaned over her.

"We aren't married. . . . Not a damn thing has been settled between us," he announced, as though this should be shocking news.

Carol said nothing, but she casually slipped her hand around the side of his neck, urging his mouth down to hers. She met with no resistance.

"Make love to me," she murmured.

Steve groaned, twisted around and dropped to sit on the side of the bed, granting her a full view of his solid back. The thread of disappointment that wrapped itself around Carol's heart was followed by a slow, lazy smile that spread over her mouth as she recognized his frantic movements.

Steve was undressing.

Feeling deliciously warm and content, Carol woke two hours later to the sound of Steve rummaging in the kitchen. No doubt he was looking for something to eat. Smiling, she jerked her arms high above her head and stretched. She yawned and arched her back, slightly elevating her hips with the action. She felt marvelous. Stupendous. Happy.

Her heart bursting with newfound joy, she reached for Steve's shirt and purposely buttoned it just enough to be provocative while looking as if she'd made some effort to cover herself.

Semiclothed, she moved toward the noise emanating from her kitchen. Barefoot, dressed only in his slacks, Steve was bent over, investigating the contents of her refrigerator.

Carol paused in the doorway. "Making love always did make you hungry," she said from behind him.

"There's hardly a damn thing in here except sweet potatoes. Good grief, woman, what are you doing with all these leftover yams?"

Carol felt sudden heat rise in her cheeks as hurried excuses crowded her mind. "They were on sale this week because of Christmas."

"They must have been at rock-bottom price. I counted six containers full of them. It looks like you've been eating them at every meal for an entire week."

"There's some pie if that'll interest you," she said, a little too quickly. "And plenty of turkey for a sandwich, if you want."

He straightened, closed the refrigerator and turned to face her. But whatever he'd intended to say apparently left him when he caught sight of her seductive pose. She was leaning against the doorjamb, hands behind her back and one foot braced against the wall, smiling at him, certain he could read her thoughts.

"There's pumpkin, and the whipped topping is fresh."

"Pumpkin?" he repeated.

"The pie."

He blinked, and nodded. "That sounds good."

"Would you like me to make you a sandwich while I'm at it?"

"Sure." But he didn't sound sure of anything at the moment.

Moving with ease around her kitchen, Carol brought out the necessary ingredients and quickly put together a snack for both of them. When she'd finished, she carried their plates to the small table across from the stove.

"Would you like something to drink?" she asked, setting their plates down.

"I'll get it," Steve said, apparently eager to help. "What would you like?"

"Milk," she responded automatically. She'd never been overly fond of the beverage but had recently made a habit of drinking a glass or two each day in preparation for her pregnancy.

"I thought you didn't like milk."

"I . . . I've acquired new tastes in the past year."

Steve grinned. "There are certain things about you that haven't changed, and then there's something more, something completely unexpected. Good God, woman, you've turned into a little she-devil, haven't you?"

Carol lowered her gaze and felt the heated blush work its way up her neck and spill into her cheeks. It wasn't any wonder Steve was teasing her. She'd been as hot as a stick of dynamite. By the time he'd undressed, she'd behaved like a tigress, clawing at him, driven by mindless passion.

Chuckling, Steve delivered two glasses of milk to the table. "You surprised me," he said. "You used to be a tad more timid."

Doing her best to ignore him, Carol brought her feet up to the edge of the chair and pulled the shirt down over her legs. With feigned dignity, she reached for half of her sandwich. "An officer and a gentleman wouldn't remind me of my wicked ways."

Still grinning, Steve lounged against the back of the chair. "You used to be far more subtle."

"Steve," she cried, "stop talking about it. Can't you see you're embarrassing me?"

"I remember one time when we were on our way to an admiral's dinner party and you casually announced you'd been in such a rush that you'd forgotten to put on any underwear."

Carol closed her eyes and looked away, remembering the time as clearly as if it had been last week instead of several years ago. She remembered, too, how good the lovemaking had been later that same evening.

"There wasn't time for us to go back to the house, so all night while you strolled around, sipping champagne, chatting and looking sedately prim, only I knew differently. Every time you looked at me, I about went crazy."

"I wanted you to know how much I longed to make love. If you'll recall, you'd just returned from a three-month tour."

"Carol, if *you'll* recall, we'd spent the entire day in bed."

She took a sip of her milk, then slowly raised her gaze to meet his. "It wasn't enough."

Steve closed his eyes and shook his head before grudgingly admitting, "It wasn't enough for me, either."

As soon as it had been socially acceptable to do so, Steve had made their excuses to the admiral that night and they'd hurriedly left the party. The entire way home, he'd been furious with Carol, telling her he was certain someone must have known what little trick she was playing. Just as heatedly, Carol had told Steve she didn't care who knew. If some huffy admiral wanted to throw a dinner party he shouldn't do it so soon after his men return from deployment.

They'd ended up making love twice that evening.

"Steve," Carol whispered with ragged emotion.

"Yes?"

"Once wasn't enough tonight, either." She dared not look at him, dared not let him see the way her pulse was clamoring.

Abruptly he stopped eating, and when he

swallowed, it looked as if he'd downed the sandwich whole. A full minute passed before he spoke.

"Not for me, either."

Their lovemaking was different this time. Unique. Unrepeatable. Earlier, it'd been like spontaneous combustion. This time was slow, easy, relaxed. Steve led her into the bedroom, unfastened the buttons of the shirt that she was wearing and let it drop unheeded to the floor.

Carol stood before him tall and proud, her taut nipples seeming to beg for his lips. Steve looked at her naked body as if seeing her for the first time. Tenderly he raised his hand to her face and brushed back a wisp of blond hair, his touch light, gentle. Then he lowered his hands and cupped the undersides of her breasts, as though weighing them in a delicate measure. The velvet stroke of his thumbs worked across her nipples until they pebbled to a throbbing hardness. From there he slid the tips of his fingers down her rib cage, grazing her heated flesh wherever he touched her.

All the while, his dark, mesmerizing gaze never left hers, as though he half expected her to protest or to stop him.

Carol felt as if her hands were being manipulated like a puppet's as she reached for his belt buckle. All she knew was that she wanted him to make love to her. Her fingers fumbled at first, unfamiliar with the workings of his belt, then managed to release the clasp.

57

Soon Steve was nude.

She studied him, awed by his strength and beauty. She wanted to tell him all that she was feeling, all the good things she sensed in him, but the words withered on her tongue as he reached out and touched her once more.

His hand continued downward from her rib cage, momentarily pausing over her flat, smooth stomach, then moving lower until it encountered her pelvis. Slowly, methodically, he braced the heel of his hand against the apex of her womanhood and started a circling, gyrating motion while his fingers explored between her parted thighs.

Hardly able to breathe, Carol opened herself more to him, and once she had, he delicately parted her and slipped one finger inside. Her eyes widened at the stab of pleasure that instantly sliced through her and she bit into her lower lip to keep from panting.

She must have made some kind of sound because Steve paused and asked, "Did I hurt you?"

Carol was incapable of any verbal response. Frantically she shook her head, and his finger continued its deft movements, quickly bringing her to an exploding release. Wave upon wave of seething spasms, each one stronger, each one more intense, overtook every part of her. Whimpering noises escaped from deep within her throat as she climaxed, and the sound propelled Steve into action.

He wrapped his arms around her and carried her to the bed, laying her on top of the rumpled sheets. Not allowing her time to alter her position or rearrange the sheets, Steve moved over her, parted her thighs and quickly impaled her.

His breathing was ragged, barely under control.

Carol's wasn't any more even.

He didn't move, torturing her with an intense longing she had never experienced. Her body was still tingling in the aftermath of one fulfillment and reaching, striving toward another. Her whole person seemed to be filled with anxious expectancy . . . waiting for something she couldn't define.

Taking her hands, Steve lifted them above her head and held them prisoner there. He leaned over her, bracing himself on his arms on either side of her head. The action thrust him deeper inside Carol. She moaned and thrashed her head against the mattress, then lifted her hips, jerking them a couple of times, seeking more.

"Not yet, love," he whispered and placed a hand under her head, lifting her mouth to his. Their kiss was wild and passionate, as though their mouths couldn't give or take enough to satisfy their throbbing need.

Steve shifted his position and completely withdrew his body from hers.

Carol felt as if she'd suddenly gone blind; the whole world seemed black and lifeless. She started to protest, started to cry out, but before the sound escaped her throat, Steve sank his manhood back inside her. A shaft of pure light filled her senses once more and she sighed audibly, relieved. She was whole again, free.

"Now," Steve told her. "Now." He moved eagerly then, in deep, calculated strokes, plunging into her again and again, gifting her with the sun, revealing the heavens, exploring the universe. Soon all Carol knew was this insistent warm friction and the sweet, indescribable pangs of pleasure. Her body trembled as ripple after ripple of deep, pure sensation pulsed over her, driving her crazy as she remembered what had nightly been hers.

Breathless, Steve moved to lie beside her, bringing her into the circle of his arms. An hour passed, it seemed, before he spoke. "Was it always this good?"

The whispered question was so low Carol had to strain to hear him. "Yes," she answered after a long, timeless moment. "Always."

He pressed his forehead against the top of her head and moaned. "I was afraid of that."

The next thing Carol was aware of was a muffled curse and the unsettling sound of something heavy crashing to the floor.

"Steve?" she sat up in bed and reached for a sheet to cover her nakedness. The room was dark and still. Dread filled her — it couldn't be morning. Not yet, not so soon.

"I'm sorry. I didn't mean to wake you."

"You're leaving?" She sent her hand searching for the lamp on the nightstand. It clicked and a muted light filled the room.

"I've got the watch today," he reminded her.

"What time is it?"

"Carol, listen," he said gruffly, "I didn't mean for any of this to happen." All the while he was speaking, Steve's fingers were working the buttons of his shirt and having little success in getting it to fasten properly. "Call what happened last night what you will — the holiday spirit, a momentary slip in my better judgment . . . whatever. I'm sure you feel the same way." He paused and turned to study her.

She leaned forward, resting her chin on her raised knees. Her heart was in her throat, and she felt shaken and miserable. "Yes, of course."

His mouth thinned and he turned his back to her once more. "I thought as much. The best thing we can do is put the entire episode out of our minds."

"Right," she answered, forcing some enthusiasm into her voice. It was working out exactly as she'd planned it: they would both wake up in the morning, feel chagrined, make their apologies and go their separate ways once more.

Only it didn't feel the way she'd anticipated. It felt wrong. Very wrong.

Steve was in the living room before she moved from the bed. Grabbing a thin robe from her closet, she slipped into it as she rushed after him.

He seemed to be waiting for her, pacing the entryway. He combed his fingers through his hair a couple of times before turning to look at her.

"So you want to forget last night?" he asked.

"I . . . if you do," she answered.

"I do."

Carol's world toppled for a moment, then quickly righted itself. She understood — it was better this way. "Thank you for the poinsettia and candy." It seemed inappropriate to mention the terrific lovemaking.

"Right." His answer was clipped, as though he was eager to be on his way. "Thanks for the dinner . . . and everything else."

"No problem." Stepping around him, Carol opened the door. "It was good to see you again, Steve."

"Yeah, you, too."

He walked out of the house and down the steps, and watching him go did crazy things to Carol's equilibrium. Suddenly she had to lean against the doorjamb just to remain upright. Something inside her, something strong and more powerful than her own will demanded that she stop him.

"Steve," she cried frantically. She stood on tiptoe. "Steve."

He turned around abruptly.

They stared at each other, each battle scarred and weary, each hurting. Each proud.

"Merry Christmas," she said softly.

"Merry Christmas."

Three days after Christmas, Carol was convinced her plan had worked perfectly. Thursday morning she woke feeling sluggish and sick to her stomach. A book she'd been reading on pregnancy and childbirth stated that the best way to relieve those early bouts of morning sickness was to nibble on soda crackers first thing — even before getting out of bed.

A burning sense of triumph led her into the bathroom, where she stared at herself in the mirror as though her reflection would proudly announce she was about to become a mother.

It had been so easy. Simple really. One tempestuous night of passion and the feat was accomplished. Her hand rested over her abdomen, and she patted it gently, feeling both proud and awed. A new life was being nurtured there.

A baby. Steve's child.

The wonder of it produced a ready flow of emotion and tears dampened her eyes.

Another symptom!

The book had explained that her emotions could be affected by the pregnancy — that she might be more susceptible to tears.

Wiping the moisture from the corners of her eyes, Carol strolled into the kitchen and searched the cupboard for saltines. She found a stale package and forced herself to eat two, but she didn't feel any better than she had earlier.

Not bothering to dress, she turned on the

television and made herself a bed on the sofa. Boeing workers were given the week between Christmas and New Year's off as part of their employment package. Carol had planned to spend the free time painting the third bedroom — the one she planned to use for the baby. Unfortunately she didn't have any energy. In fact, she felt downright sick, as though she were coming down with a case of the flu.

A lazy smile turned up the edges of her mouth. She wasn't about to complain. Nine months from now, she would be holding a precious bundle in her arms.

Steve's and her child.

Chapter Four

With his hands cupped behind his head, Steve lay in bed and stared blindly at the dark ceiling. He couldn't sleep. For the past hour he hadn't even bothered to close his eyes. It wouldn't do any good; every time he did, the memory of Christmas Eve with Carol filled his mind.

Releasing a slow breath, he rubbed his hand down his face, hoping the action would dispel her image from his thoughts. It didn't work. Nothing did.

He had never intended to make love to her, and even now, ten days later, he wasn't sure how the hell it had happened. He continued to suffer from a low-grade form of shock. His thoughts had been in utter chaos since that night, and he wasn't sure how to respond to her or where their relationship was headed now.

What really distressed him, Steve realized, was that after everything that had happened between them, he could still want her so much. More than a week later and the memory of her leaning against the doorjamb in the kitchen, wearing his shirt — and nothing else — had the power to tighten his loins. Tighten his loins! He nearly laughed out loud; that had to be the understatement of the year.

When Carol had stood and held out her arms

to him, he'd acted like a starving child offered candy, so eager he hadn't stopped to think about anything except the love she would give him. Any protest he'd made had been token. She'd volunteered, he'd accepted, and that should be the end of it.

But it wasn't.

Okay, so he wasn't a man of steel. Carol had always been his Achilles' heel, and he knew it. She knew it. In thinking over the events of that night, it was almost as though his ex-wife had planned everything. Her red dress with no bra, and that bit about placing decorations on the tree. She'd insisted on standing on the chair, stretching and exposing her thigh to him . . . his thoughts came to a skidding halt.

No.

He wasn't going to fall into that familiar trap of thinking Carol was using him, deceiving him. It did no good to wade into the muddy mire of anger, bitterness, regret and doubt.

He longed to repress the memory of Carol's warm and willing body in his arms. If only he could get on with his life. If only he could sleep.

He couldn't.

His sister, Lindy, had coffee brewed by the time Steve came out of his bedroom. She sat at the table, cradling a cup in one hand while holding a folded section of the *Post-Intelligencer* in the other.

"Morning." She glanced up and greeted him

with a bright smile. Lately it seemed his sister was always smiling.

Steve mumbled something unintelligible as a means of reply. Her cheerfulness grated against him. He wasn't in the mood for good humor this morning. He wasn't in the mood for anything . . . with the possible exception of making love to Carol again, and that bit of insight didn't suit him in the least.

"It doesn't look like you had a good night's sleep, brother dearest."

Steve's frown deepened, and he gave his sister another noncommittal answer.

"I don't suppose this has anything to do with Carol?" She waited, and when he didn't answer, added, "Or the fact that you didn't come home Christmas Eve?"

"I came home."

"Sure, sometime the following morning."

Steve took down a mug from the cupboard and slapped it against the counter with unnecessary force. "Drop it, Lindy. I don't want to discuss Carol."

A weighted silence followed his comment.

"Rush and I've got almost everything ready to move into the new apartment," she offered finally, and the light tone of her voice suggested she was looking for a way to put their conversation back on an even keel. "We'll be out of here by Friday."

Hell, here he was snapping at Lindy. His sister didn't deserve to be the brunt of his foul

67

mood. She hadn't done anything but mention the obvious. "Speaking of Rush, where is he?" Steve asked, forcing a lighter tone into his own voice.

"He had to catch an early ferry this morning," she said, and hesitated momentarily. "I'm happy, Steve, really happy. I was so afraid for a time that I'd made a dreadful mistake, but I know now that marrying Rush was the right thing to do."

Steve took a sip of coffee to avoid looking at his sister. What Lindy was actually saying was that she wanted him to find the same contentment she had. That wasn't possible for him now, and wouldn't be until he got Carol out of his blood.

And making love to her Christmas Eve hadn't helped.

"Well, I suppose I should think about getting dressed," Lindy said with a heavy dose of feigned enthusiasm. "I'm going to get some boxes so Rush and I can finish up the last of the packing."

"Where's your new apartment?" Steve had been so preoccupied with his own troubles that he hadn't thought to inquire until now.

As Lindy rattled off the address Steve's forehead furrowed into a brooding frown. His sister and Rush were moving less than a mile away from Carol's place. Great! That was the last thing he needed to hear.

Steve's day wasn't much better than his

sleepless night had been. By noon he'd decided he could no longer avoid the inevitable. He didn't like it, but it was necessary.

He had to talk to Carol.

He was thankful the apartment was empty when he arrived home shortly after six. Not willing to test his good fortune, and half expecting Lindy or Rush to appear at any minute, he walked directly to the phone and punched out Carol's number as though punishing the telephone would help relieve some of his nervousness.

"Hello?" Carol's soft, lilting voice clawed at his abdomen.

"It's Steve."

A pregnant pause was followed by a slightly breathless "Hi."

"I was thinking we should talk."

"All right." She sounded surprised, pleased, uncertain. "When?"

Steve rotated his wrist and looked at the time. "What are you doing right now?"

She hesitated. "I . . . nothing."

Although slightly awkward, their conversation to this point had felt right to Steve. But the way she paused, as though searching for a delaying tactic, troubled him. Fiery arrows of doubt hit their mark and he said, "Listen, Carol, if you're 'entertaining' Todd, I'd prefer to stop by later."

The ensuing silence was more deafening than jungle drums pounding out a war chant.

It took her several seconds to answer him, and when she did, the soft voice that had greeted him was racked with pain. "You can come now."

Steve tightened his hold on the phone receiver in a punishing grip. He hated it when he talked to her like that. He didn't know who he was punishing: Carol or himself. "I'll be there in fifteen minutes."

Carol replaced the telephone in its cradle and battled down an attack of pain and tears. How dare Steve suggest Todd was there. Suddenly she was so furious with him that she could no longer stand in one place. She started pacing the living room floor like a raw recruit, taking five or six steps and then doing an abrupt about-face. And yet she was excited — even elated.

Steve had taken the initiative to contact her, and it proved that he hadn't been able to stop thinking about her, either.

Nothing had been right for her since Christmas Eve. Oh, she'd reached her objective — exceeded it. Everything had gone according to plan. Only Carol hadn't counted on the doubts and bewilderment that had followed their night of loving. Their short hours together brought back the memory of how good their lives had once been, how much they'd loved each other and how happy those first years were.

Since Christmas Eve, Carol had been crippled with "if onlys" and "what ifs," tossing around those weak phrases as though she expected them to alter reality. Each day it became more difficult to remember that Steve had divorced her, that he believed her capable of the worst kind of deception. One night in his arms and she was fool enough to be willing to forget all the pain of the past thirteen months.

Almost willing, she amended.

It took vindictive, destructive comments like the one he'd just made to remind her that they had a rocky road to travel if they hoped to salvage their relationship.

Before Steve arrived, Carol had time to freshen her makeup and run a brush through her thick blond hair. She paused to study her reflection in the mirror and wondered if he would ever guess her secret. She doubted it. If he couldn't read the truth in her eyes about Todd, then he wasn't likely to recognize her joy, or guess the cause.

Thinking about the baby helped lighten the weight of Steve's bitterness. Briefly she closed her eyes and imagined holding that precious bundle in her arms. A little girl, she decided, with dark brown eyes like Steve's and soft blond curls.

The mental picture of her child made everything seem worthwhile.

When the doorbell chimed, Carol was ready. She held the door open for Steve and even managed to greet him with a smile.

"I made coffee."

"Good." His answer was gruff, as though he were speaking to one of his enlisted men.

He followed her into the kitchen and stood silently as she poured them each a cup of coffee. When she turned around, she saw Steve standing with his hands in his pockets, looking unsettled and ill at ease.

"If you're searching for traces of Todd, let me tell you right now, you won't find any."

He had the good grace to look mildly chagrined. "I suppose I should apologize for that remark."

"I suppose I should accept." She pulled out a chair and sat.

Steve claimed the one directly across from her.

Neither spoke, and it seemed to Carol that an eternity passed. "You wanted to talk to me," she said, after what felt like two lifetimes.

"I'm not exactly sure what I want to say."

She smiled a little at that, understanding. "I'm not sure what I want to hear, either."

A hint of a grin bounced from his dark eyes. "Forgiving you for what happened with Todd . . ."

Carol bolted to her feet with such force that her chair nearly fell backward. "Forgiving me!" she demanded, shaking with outrage.

"Carol, please, I didn't come here to fight."

"Then don't start one. Don't come into my home and hurl insults at me. The one person in

72

this room who should be seeking forgiveness is *you!*"

"Carol . . ."

"I should have known this wouldn't work, but like a lovesick fool I thought . . . I hoped you . . ." She paused, jerked her head around and rubbed the heels of her hands down her cheeks, erasing the telltale tears.

"Okay, I apologize. I won't mention Todd again."

She inhaled a wobbly breath and nodded, not trusting her voice, and sat back down.

Another awkward moment followed.

"I don't know what you've been thinking, or how you feel about . . . what happened," Steve said, "but for the past ten days, I've felt like a leaf caught in a windstorm. My emotions are in turmoil . . . I can't stop remembering how good it was between us, and how right it felt to have you in my arms again. My instincts tell me that night was a fluke, and best forgotten. I just wish to hell I could."

Carol bowed her head, avoiding eye contact. "I've been thinking the same thing. As you said when you left, we should chalk it up to the love and goodwill that's synonymous with the season. But the holidays are over and I can't stop thinking about it, either."

"The loving always was terrific, wasn't it?"

He didn't sound as though he wanted to admit even that much, as if he preferred to discount anything positive about their lives together. Carol understood the impulse. She'd done the same thing since their divorce; it helped ease the pain of the separation.

Grudgingly she nodded. "Unfortunately the lovemaking is only a small part of any marriage. I think Christmas Eve gave me hope that you and I might be able to work everything out. I'd like to resolve the past and find a way to heal the wounds." They'd been apart for over a year, but Carol's heart felt as bloodied and bruised as if their divorce had been decreed yesterday.

"God knows, I want to forget the past . . ."

Hope clamored in her breast and she raised her eyes to meet Steve's, but his gaze was as weary and doubtful as her own.

His eyes fell. "But I don't think I can. I don't know if I'll ever be able to get over finding Todd in our bedroom."

"He was in the shower," Carol corrected through clenched teeth. "And the only reason he was there was because the shower head in the other bathroom wasn't working properly."

"What the hell difference does it make?" Steve shouted. "He spent the night here. You've never bothered to deny that."

"But nothing happened . . . if you'd stayed long enough to ask Todd, he would have explained."

"If I'd stayed any longer, I would have killed him."

He said it with such conviction that Carol didn't doubt him. Long before, she'd promised herself she wouldn't defend her actions again. Todd had been her employer and her friend. She'd known Todd and his wife, Joyce, were having marital troubles. But she cared about them both and didn't want to get caught in the middle of their problems. Todd, however, had cast her there when he showed up on her doorstep, drunk out of his mind, wanting to talk. Alarmed, Carol had brought him inside and phoned Joyce, who suggested Todd sleep it off at Carol's house. It had seemed like a reasonable solution, although she wasn't keen on the idea. Steve was away and due back to Seattle in a couple of days.

But Steve had arrived home early — and assumed the worst.

The sadness that settled over her was profound, and when she spoke, her voice was little more than a whisper. "You tried and found me guilty on circumstantial evidence, Steve. For the first couple of weeks, I tried to put myself in your place . . . I could understand how you read the scene that morning, but you were wrong."

It looked for a moment as though he was going to argue with her. She could almost see the wheels spinning in his mind, stirring up the doubts, building skyscrapers on sand foundations.

"Other things started to add up," he admitted reluctantly, still not looking at her.

Carol could all but see him close his mind to

common sense. It seemed that just when they were beginning to make headway, Steve would pull something else into their argument or make some completely ridiculous comment that made absolutely no sense to her. The last time they'd tried to discuss this in a reasonable, nonconfrontational manner, Steve had hinted that she'd been Todd's lover for months. He'd suggested that she hadn't been as eager to welcome him home from his last cruise, which was ridiculous. They may have had problems, but none had extended to the bedroom.

"What 'other things' do you mean now?" she asked, defeat coating her words.

He ignored her question. His mouth formed a cocky smile, devoid of amusement. "I will say one thing for ol' Todd — he taught you well."

She gasped at the unexpected pain his words inflicted.

Steve paled and looked away. "I shouldn't have said that — I didn't mean it."

"Todd did teach me," she countered, doing her best to keep her bottom lip from quivering. "He taught me that a marriage not based on mutual trust isn't worth the ink that prints the certificate. He taught me that it takes more than a few words murmured by a man of God to make a relationship work."

"That's not what I meant."

"I know what you meant. Your jealousy has you tied up in such tight knots that you're incapable of reasoning any of this out."

Steve ignored that comment. "I'm not jealous of Todd — he can have you if he wants."

Carol thought she was going to be sick to her stomach. Indignation filled her throat, choking off any possible reply.

Steve stood and walked across the kitchen, his hands knotted into fists at his sides. He closed his eyes briefly, and when he opened them, he looked like a stranger, his inner torment was so keen.

"I didn't mean that," he said unevenly. "I don't know why I say such ugly things to you."

Carol heard the throb of pain in her voice. "I don't know why you do, either. If you're trying to hurt me, then congratulations. You've succeeded beyond your expectations."

Steve stood silently a few moments, then delivered his untouched coffee to the sink. His hesitation surprised Carol. She'd assumed he would walk out — that was the way their arguments usually ended.

Instead he turned to face her and asked, "Are Todd and Joyce still married?"

She'd gotten a Christmas card from them a couple of weeks earlier. Until she'd seen both their names at the bottom of the greeting, she hadn't been sure if their marriage had weathered better than hers and Steve's. "They're still together."

Steve frowned and nodded. "I know that makes everything more difficult for you."

"Stop it, Steve!" This new list of questions irritated her almost as much as his tireless insinuations. "All the years we were married, not once did I accuse you of being unfaithful, even though you were gone half the time."

"It's difficult to find a woman willing to fool around 400 feet under water."

"That's not my point. I trusted you. I always did, and I assumed that you trusted me, too. That's all I've ever asked of you, all I ever wanted."

He was quiet for so long that Carol wondered if he'd chosen to ignore her rather than come up with an appropriate answer.

"You didn't discover another woman lounging around in a see-through nightie while I showered, either. You may be able to explain away some of what happened, but as far as I'm concerned there are gaping holes in your story."

Carol clenched her teeth so tightly that her jaw ached. She'd already broken a promise to herself by discussing Todd with Steve. When the divorce was final, Carol had determined then that no amount of justifying would ever satisfy her ex-husband. Discussing Todd had yet to settle a single problem, and in the end she only hurt herself.

"I don't think we're going to solve anything by rehashing this now," she told him calmly. "Unless our love is firmly grounded in a foundation of trust, there's no use even trying to work things out."

"It doesn't seem to be helping, does it? I wanted us —"

"I know," she interrupted softly, sadly. "I wanted it, too. The other night only served to remind us how much we'd loved each other."

They shared a discouraged smile, and Carol felt as though her heart was breaking in half.

He took a few steps toward the front door. "I'll be leaving in less than three weeks."

"How long will you be away?" For a long time she hadn't felt comfortable asking him this kind of question, but he seemed more open to discussion now.

"Three months." He buried his hands in his pockets and Carol got the impression that the action was to keep him from reaching for her and kissing her goodbye. He paused, turned toward her and said, "If you need anything . . ."

"I won't."

Her answer didn't appear to please him. "No, I don't suppose you will. You always could take care of yourself. I used to be proud of you for being so capable, but it intimidated me, too."

"What do you mean?"

He hedged, as if searching his reserve of memories to find the perfect example, then shook his head. "Never mind, it isn't important now."

Carol walked him to the front door, her heart heavy. "I wish it could be different for us."

"I do, too."

Steve stood, unmoving, in the entryway. Inches from him, Carol felt an inner yearning more potent than anything she'd ever experienced engulf her, filling her heart with regret. Once more she would have to watch the man she loved walk away from her. Once more she must freely allow him to go.

Steve must have sensed the intense longing, because he gently rested his hands on the curve of her shoulders. She smiled and tilted her chin toward him, silently offering him her mouth.

Slowly, without hurry, Steve lowered his face to hers, drawing out each second as though he were relaxing a hold on his considerable pride, admitting his need to kiss her. It was as if he had to prove, if only to himself, that he had control of the situation.

Then his mouth grazed hers. Lightly. Briefly. Coming back for more when it became apparent the teasing kisses weren't going to satisfy either of them.

What shocked Carol most was the gentleness of his kiss. He touched and held her as he would a delicate piece of porcelain, slipping his arms around her waist, drawing her close against him.

He broke off the kiss and Carol tucked her forehead against his chest. "Have a safe trip." Silently she prayed for his protection and that he would come back to her.

"If you want, I'll phone when I return. That is . . . if you think I should?"

Maybe she could tell him about the baby then, depending on how things went between them. "Yes, by all means, phone and let me know that you made it back in one piece."

His gaze centered on her mouth and again he bent his head toward her. This time his kiss was hungry, lingering, insistent. Carol whimpered when his tongue, like a soft flame, entered her mouth, sending hot sparks of desire shooting up her spine. Her knees weakened and she nearly collapsed when Steve abruptly released her.

"For once, maybe you could miss me," he said, with a sad note of bitterness.

The following morning, Carol woke feeling queasy. It'd been that way almost since Christmas morning. She reached for the two soda crackers on the nightstand and nibbled on them before climbing out of bed. Her hand rested lovingly on her flat stomach.

She'd wanted to schedule an appointment with the doctor, but the receptionist had told her to wait until her monthly cycle was a week late. She was only overdue by a day, but naturally she wouldn't be having her period. As far as Carol was concerned, another week was too long to wait, even if she was certain she bore the desired fruit from her night with Steve.

In an effort to confirm what she already knew, Carol had purchased a home-pregnancy test. Now she climbed out of bed, read the instructions through twice, did what the package told her and waited.

The waiting was the worst part. Thirty minutes had never seemed to take so long.

Humming a catchy tune, she dressed for work, poured herself a glass of milk, then went back to the bathroom to read the test results.

She felt so cocky, so sure of what the test would tell her that her heart was already pounding with excitement.

The negative reading claimed her breath. She blinked, certain she'd misread it.

Stunned, she sat on the edge of the bathtub and took several deep breaths. She started to tremble, and tears of disappointment filled her eyes. She must be pregnant — she had to be. All the symptoms were there — everything she'd read had supported her belief.

Once more she examined the test results.

Negative.

After everything she'd gone through, after all the sweet potatoes she'd forced down her throat, after the weeks of planning, the plotting, the scheduling . . .

There wasn't going to be any baby. There never had been. Her plan had failed.

There was only one thing left to do.

Try again.

Chapter Five

It took courage for Carol to drive to Steve's apartment. Someone should award medals for this brand of lionheartedness, she murmured to herself — although she was more interested in playing the role of a tigress than a lion. If this second venture was anything like the first, Steve wouldn't know what hit him. At least, she hoped he wouldn't guess.

She straightened her shoulders, pinched some color into her cheeks and pasted on a smile. Then she rang the doorbell.

To say Steve looked surprised to see her when he opened the door would be an understatement, Carol acknowledged. His eyes rounded, his mouth relaxed and fell open, and for a moment he was utterly speechless. "Carol?"

"I suppose I should have phoned first . . ."

"No, come in." He stepped aside so that she could enter the apartment.

Beyond his obvious astonishment, Carol found it difficult to read Steve's reaction. She stepped inside gingerly, praying that her plastic smile wouldn't crack. The first thing she noticed was the large picture window in the living room, offering an unobstructed view of the Seattle waterfront. It made Elliott Bay seem close, so vivid that she could almost smell the sea-weed and feel the salty spray in the air. A large green-and-white ferry boat plowed its way through the dark waters, enhancing the picture.

"Oh . . . this is nice." Carol turned around to face him. "Have you lived here long?"

He nodded. "Rush had the apartment first. I moved in after you and I split and sort of inherited it when Rush and Lindy moved into their own place recently."

The last thing Carol wanted to remind him of was their divorce, and she quickly steered the conversation to the reason for her visit. "I found something I thought might be yours," she said hurriedly, fumbling with the snap of her eel-skin purse to bring out the button. It was a weak excuse, but she was desperate. Retrieving the small gray button from inside her coin purse, she handed it over to him.

Steve's brow pleated into a frown and he stiffened. "No . . . this isn't mine. It must belong to another man," he said coldly.

A bad move, Carol realized, taking back the button. "There's only been one man at my house, and that's you," she said, trying to stay calm. "If it isn't yours, then it must have fallen off something of my own."

Hands in his pockets, Steve nodded.

An uneasy pause followed.

Steve didn't suggest she take off her coat, didn't offer her any refreshment or any excuse to linger. Feeling crestfallen and defeated,

Carol knew there was nothing more to do but leave.

"Well, I suppose I should think about getting myself some dinner. There's a new Mexican restaurant close to here I thought I might try," she said with feigned enthusiasm, and glanced up at him through thick lashes. Steve loved enchiladas, and she prayed he would take the bait. God knew, she couldn't have been any more obvious had she issued the invitation straight out.

"I ate earlier," he announced starkly.

Steve rarely had dinner before six. He was either wise to her ways or lying.

"I see." She took a step toward the exit, wondering what else she could do to delay the inevitable. "When does the *Atlantis* leave?"

"Monday."

Three days. She had only three days to carry out her plan. Three days to get him into bed and convince him it was all his idea. Three miserable days. Her fingers curled into impotent fists of frustration inside her coat pocket.

"Have a safe trip, Steve," she said softly. "I'll . . . I'll be thinking of you."

It had been a mistake to come to his place, a mistake not to have plotted the evening more carefully. It was apparent from the stiff way Steve treated her, he couldn't wait to get her out of his apartment. Since it was Friday night, he might have a date. The thought of Steve with another woman produced a gut-wrenching

85

pain that she did her best to ignore. Dropping by unexpectedly like this wasn't helping her cause.

She'd hoped they could make love tonight. Her temperature was elevated and she was as fertile as she was going to get this month.

Swallowing her considerable pride, she paused, her hand on the door handle. "There's a new spy thriller showing at the Fifth Avenue Theater. . . . You always used to like espionage films."

Steve's eyes narrowed as he studied her. It was difficult for Carol to meet his heated gaze and not wilt from sheer nerves. She was sure her cheeks were hot pink. Coming to his apartment was the most difficult thing she'd done in years. Her heart felt as if it was going to hammer its way right out of her chest, and her fingers were shaking so badly that she didn't dare remove them from her pockets.

"Why are you here?" His question was soft, suspicious, uncertain.

"I found the button." One glance told her he didn't believe her, as well he shouldn't. That excuse was so weak it wouldn't carry feathers.

"What is it you *really* want, Carol?"

"I . . . I . . ." Her voice trembled from her lips, and her heart, which had been pounding so furiously a second before, seemed to stop completely. She swallowed and forced her gaze to meet his before dropping it. When she finally managed to speak, her voice was low and mean-

ingful. "I thought with you going away. . . ."
Good grief, woman, her mind shouted, quit
playing games. Give him the truth.

She raised her chin, and her gaze locked with
his. "I'm not wearing any underwear."

Steve went stock-still, holding his jaw tight
and hard. The inner conflict that played over
his face was as vivid as the picturesque scene
she'd viewed from his living-room window. The
few feet of distance between them seemed to
stretch wider than a mile.

It felt as if an eternity passed as Carol waited
for his reaction, and she felt paralyzed with
misgivings. She'd exposed her hand and left her
pride completely vulnerable to him.

She saw it then — a flicker of his eyes, a
movement in the line of his jaw, a softening in
his tightly controlled facial features. He wanted
her, too — wanted her with a desperation that
made him as weak as she was. Her heart leaped
wildly with joy.

Steve lifted his hand and held it out to her,
and Carol thought she would collapse with relief as she hurried toward him. He crushed her
in his arms and his mouth hungrily came down
on hers. His eager lips smothered her cry of
happiness. Equally greedy, Carol returned his
kiss, reveling in his embrace. She twined her
arms around his neck, her softness melding
against the hardened contours of his body.

His hands tightened around her possessively,
stroking her spine, then lowered over the

rounded firmness of her buttocks. He gathered her pelvis as close to him as was humanly possible.

"Dear God, I've gone crazy."

Carol raised her hands to frame his face and gazed lovingly into his eyes. "Me, too," she whispered before spreading a circle of light kisses over his forehead, chin and mouth.

"I shouldn't be doing this."

"Yes, you should."

Steve groaned and clasped her tighter. He kissed her, plunging his tongue into the sweet softness of her mouth, exploring it with a desperate urgency. Carol met his tongue with her own in a silent duel that left them both exhausted.

While they were still kissing, Steve unfastened the buttons of her coat, slipped it from her shoulders and dropped it to the floor. His hands clawed at the back of her skirt, lifting it away from her legs, then settled once again, cupping her bare bottom.

He moaned, his breath seemed to jam in his throat, and his eyes darkened with passion. "You weren't kidding."

Carol bit her lower lip as a wealth of sensation fired through her from the touch of his cool hands against her heated flesh. She rotated her lower body shamelessly against the rigid evidence of his desire.

His hands closed over her breasts and her nipples rose as though to greet him, to welcome him. His eager but uncooperative fingers fiddled with the fastenings of her blouse. Smiling, content but just as eager, Carol gently brushed his hands aside and completed the task for him. He pulled the silk material free of her waistline and disposed of it as effectively as he had her coat. Her breasts sprang to life in his hands and when he moaned, the sound of it excited her so much that it throbbed in her ears.

The moist heat of his mouth closed over her nipple and she gasped. The exquisite pleasure nearly caused her knees to buckle. Blood roared through her veins, and liquid fire scorched her until she was certain she would soon explode. She lifted one leg and wrapped it around his thigh, anchoring her weight against him.

Steve's fingers reached for her and instinctively she opened herself to him. He teased her womanhood, toyed with her, tormented her with delicate strokes that drove her over the brink. Within seconds, she tossed back her head and groaned as the pulsating climax rocked through her, sending out rippling waves of release.

By the time Steve carried her into his bedroom, Carol was panting. He didn't waste any time, discarding his clothes with an urgency that thrilled her. When he moved to the bed, his features were keen with desire.

Carol lifted her arms to welcome him, loving him with a tenderness that came from the very marrow of her bones.

Steve shifted his weight over her and captured her mouth in a consuming kiss that sent Carol down into a whirlpool of the sweetest oblivion. Anxious and eager, she parted her thighs for him and couldn't hold back a small cry as he sheathed himself inside her, slipping the proud heat of his manhood into her moist softness.

He waited, as though to prolong the pleasure and soak in her love before he started to move. The feelings that wrapped themselves around her were so incredible that Carol had to struggle to hold back the tears. With each delicious stroke the tension mounted and slowly, methodically began to uncurl within her until she was thrashing her head against his pillow and arching her hips to meet each plunging thrust.

Steve groaned and threw back his head, struggling to regain control, but soon he, too, was over the edge. When he cried out his voice harmonized with hers in a song that was as ageless as mankind.

Breathless, he collapsed on top of her. Her arms slipped around his neck and she buried her face in the hollow of his throat, kissing him, hugging him, needing him desperately. Tears slipped silently from the corners of her eyes. They spoke the words that she couldn't, eloquently telling him of all the love buried in her heart — words Carol feared she would never be able to voice again.

When Steve moved to lift himself off of her, she wouldn't let him. She held him tightly, her fingers gripping his shoulders.

"I'm too heavy," he protested.

"No . . . hold me."

With his arms wrapped around her, he rolled over, carrying her with him in one continuous motion until their positions were reversed.

Content for the moment, Carol pressed her ear over his chest, listening to the strong, steady beat of his heart.

Neither spoke.

His hand moved up and down her spine in a tender caress as though he had to keep touching her to know she was real. Her tears slid onto his shoulder, but neither mentioned it.

In her soul, Carol had to believe that something this beautiful would create a child. At this moment everything seemed perfect and healed between them, the way it had been two years before.

Gently Steve kissed her forehead, and she snuggled closer, flattening her hands over his chest.

He wrapped his arms around her and his thumb tenderly wiped the moisture from her cheek. Tucking his finger under her chin, he lifted it enough to find her mouth and kiss her. Sweetly.

"I tried, but I never could stop loving you,"

he whispered in a voice raw with emotion. "I hated myself for being so weak, but I don't anymore."

"I'll always love you," she answered. "I can't help myself. This year has been the worst of my entire life. I've felt as if I was trapped in a freezer, never able to get warm."

"No more," he said, his eyes trapping hers.

"No more," she agreed, and her heart leaped with unleashed joy.

They rested for a full hour, their legs entwined, their arms wrapped around each other. Every now and again, Steve would kiss her, his lips playing over hers. Then Carol would kiss him back, darting her tongue in and out of his mouth and doing all the things she knew he enjoyed. She raised herself up on her elbows and brushed a thick swatch of dark hair from his brow. It felt so good to be able to touch him this freely.

"What's the name of that Mexican restaurant you mentioned earlier?" Steve asked.

Carol smiled smugly. "You are so predictable."

"How's that?"

"Making love never fails to make you hungry!"

"True," he growled into her ear, "but often my appetite isn't for food." His index finger circled her nipple, teasing it to a rose-colored pebble. "I've got a year's worth of loving stored up for you, and the way you make me feel tonight, we may never leave this bedroom."

And they didn't.

Carol woke when Steve pressed a soft kiss on her lips.

"Hmm," she said, not opening her eyes. She smiled up at him, sated and unbelievably happy. She wore the look of a woman who loves wisely and who knows that her love is returned. "Is it morning yet?"

"It was morning the last time we made love." Steve laughed and leaned over to kiss her again, as if one sample wasn't nearly enough to satisfy him.

"It was?" she asked lazily. They'd slept intermittently, waking every few hours, holding and kissing each other. While asleep, Carol would roll over and forget Steve was at her side. Their discovery each time was worth far more than a few semiprecious hours of sleep. And Steve seemed equally excited about her being there with him.

"Currently," he said, dragging her back to reality, "it's going on noon."

"Noon!" She bolted upright. She'd been in her teens the last time she'd slept this late.

"I'm sorry to wake you, honey, but I've got to get to the sub."

Carol was surprised to see that he was dressed and prepared to leave. He handed her a fresh cup of coffee, which she readily took from him. "You'll be back, won't you?"

"Not until tomorrow morning."

"Will you . . . could you stop off and see me one more time, before you leave?"

His dark gaze caressed her. "Honest to God, Carol, I don't think I could stay away."

As Steve walked away from his parked car at the Navy base in Bangor, less than ten miles north of Bremerton, he was convinced his strut would put a rooster to shame. Lord, he felt good.

Carol had come to him, wanted him, loved him as much as he'd always loved and wanted her. All the world felt good to him.

For the first time since they'd divorced, he felt whole. He'd been a crazed fool to harp on the subject of Todd Larson to Carol. From this moment on, he vowed never to mention the other man's name again. Obviously whatever had been between the two was over, and she hadn't wanted Todd back. Okay, so she'd made a mistake. Lord knew, he'd committed his share, and a lot of them had to do with Carol. He'd been wrong to think he could flippantly cast her out of his life.

In his pain, he'd lashed out at her, acted like a heel, refused to have anything to do with her because of his foolish pride. But Carol had been woman enough to forgive him. He couldn't do anything less than be man enough to forget the past. The love they shared was too precious to muddy with doubts. They'd both made mistakes, and the time had come to rec-

94

tify those and learn from them.

Dear God, he felt ready to soar. He shouldn't be on a nuclear submarine — a feeling this good was meant for rockets.

Carol found herself humming as she whipped the cream into a frothy topping for Steve's favorite dessert: French pudding. She licked her index finger, grinned lazily to herself and leaned her hip against the kitchen counter, feeling happier than she could remember being in a long time.

Friday night had been incredible. Steve had been incredible. The only cost had been her bruised pride when she'd arrived at his apartment with such a flimsy excuse. The price had been minor, the rewards major.

Not once during the entire evening had Steve mentioned Todd's name. Maybe, just maybe, he was ready to put that all behind them now.

If she was pregnant from their Friday night lovemaking, which she sincerely prayed she was, it would be best for the baby to know "her" father. Originally Carol had intended to raise the child without Steve. She wasn't sure she would ever have told him. Now the thought of suppressing the information seemed both childish and petty. But she wasn't going to use the baby as a convenient excuse for a reconciliation. They would settle matters first — then she would tell him.

Steve would make a good father; she'd

watched him around children and had often been amazed by his patience. He'd wanted a family almost from the first. Carol had been the one who'd insisted on waiting, afraid she wouldn't be able to manage her job, a home and a baby with her husband away so much of the time, although she'd never admitted it to Steve. She knew how important it was for him to believe in her strength and independence. But this past year had matured her. Now she was ready for the responsibility.

Naturally hindsight was twenty-twenty, and she regretted having put off Steve's desire to start a family. The roots of their marriage might have been strong enough to withstand what had happened if there'd been children binding them together. But it did no good to second-guess fate.

Children. Carol hadn't dared think beyond one baby. But if she and Steve were to get back together — something that was beginning to look like a distinct possibility — then they could plan on having a houseful of kids!

It was early afternoon by the time Steve made it to Carol's house. A cold wind from the north whistled through the tops of the trees and the sky was darkening with a brewing storm.

Carol tossed aside her knitting and flew across the room the minute she heard a car door close, knowing it had to be Steve. By the time he was to the porch, she had the front door open for him.

He wore his uniform, which told her he hadn't stopped off at his apartment to change. Obviously he was eager to see her again, Carol thought, immeasurably pleased.

"I'm glad to see you're waiting for me," he said, and his words formed a soft fog around his mouth. He took the steps two at a time and rubbed his bare hands together.

"I can't believe how cold it is." Carol pulled him inside the house and closed the door.

His gaze sought hers. "Warm me, then."

She didn't require a second invitation, and stood on the tips of her toes to kiss him, leaning her weight into his. Steve wrapped her in his embrace, kissing her back greedily, as if they had been apart six weeks instead of a single day. When he finished, they were both breathless.

"It feels like you missed me."

"I did," she assured him. "Give me your coat and I'll hang it up for you."

He gave her the thick wool jacket and strolled into the living room. "What's this?" he asked, looking at her knitting.

Carol's heart leaped to her throat. "A baby blanket."

"For who?"

"A . . . friend." She considered herself a friend, so that was at least a half-truth. She'd been working on the blanket in her spare time since before Christmas. It had helped her feel as if she was doing something constructive toward her goal.

Suddenly she felt as if she had a million things to tell him. "I got energetic and cleaned house. I don't know what's wrong with me lately, but I don't have the energy I used to have."

"Have you been sick?"

She loved him for the concern in his voice. "No, I'm in perfect health . . . I've just been tired lately . . . not getting enough vitamins, I suppose. But it doesn't matter now because I feel fantastic, full of ambition — I even made you French pudding."

"Carol, I think you should see a doctor."

"And if he advises bed rest, do you promise to, er . . . rest with me?"

"Good heavens, woman, you've become insatiable."

"I know." She laughed and slipped her arm around his waist. "I was always that way around you."

"Always?" he teased. "I don't seem to recall that."

"Then I'll just have to remind you." She steered him toward the bedroom, crawled onto the mattress and knelt there. "If you want French pudding, fellow, you're going to have to work for it."

The alarm went off at six. Carol blindly

reached out and, after a couple of wide swipes, managed to hit the switch that would turn off the electronic beeping.

Steve stirred at her side. "It's time," she said in a small, sad voice. This would be their last morning together for three months.

"It's six already?" Steve moaned.

"I'm afraid so."

He reached for her and brought her close to his side. His hand found hers and he laced her fingers with his. "Carol, listen, we only have a little time left and there's so much I should have said, so much I wanted to tell you."

"I wanted to talk to you, too." In all the years they were married, no parting had been less welcome. Carol yearned to wrap her arms around him and beg him not to leave her. It was times like this that she wished Steve had chosen a career outside the Navy. In a few hours he would sail out of Hood Canal, and she wouldn't hear from him for the entire length of his deployment. Other than hearsay, Carol wasn't even to know where he would be sailing. For reasons of national security, all submarine deployments were regarded as top secret.

"When I return from this tour, Carol, I'd like us to have a serious talk about getting back together. I know I've been a jerk, and you deserve someone better, but I'd like you to think about it while I'm away. Will you do that for me?"

She couldn't believe how close she was to

breaking into tears. "Yes," she whispered. "I'll think about it very seriously. I want everything to be right . . . the second time."

"I do, too." He raised her hand to his mouth and kissed her knuckles. "Another thing . . . make an appointment for a physical. I don't remember you being this thin."

"I lost fifteen pounds when we were divorced; I can't seem to gain it back." The tears broke through the surface and she sobbed out the words, ending in a hiccup. Embarrassed, she pressed her fingertips over her lips. "I've been a wreck without you, Steve Kyle . . . I suppose it makes you happy to know how miserable and lonely this past year has been."

"I was just as miserable and lonely," he admitted. "We can't allow anything to do this to us again. I love you too damn much to spend another year like the last one." His touch was so tender, so loving that she melted into his embrace.

"You have to trust me, Steve. I can't have you coming back and even suspecting I'd see another man."

"I know . . . I do trust you."

She closed her eyes at the relief his words gave her. "Thank you for that."

He kissed her then and, with a reluctance that tore at her heart, pulled away from her and started to dress.

She reached for her robe, not looking at him as she slipped her arms into the long sleeves.

100

"If we do decide to make another go at marriage, I'd like to seriously think about starting a family right away. What would you say to that?"

Steve hesitated. Carol turned around to search out his gaze in the stirring light of early morning, and the tender look he wore melted any lingering doubts she harbored.

"Just picturing you with my child in your arms," he whispered hoarsely, "is enough to keep me going for the next three months."

Chapter Six

A week after Steve sailed, Carol began experiencing symptoms that again suggested she was pregnant. The early morning bouts of nausea returned. She found herself weeping over a rerun of *Magnum, P.I.* And she was continually tired, feeling worn-out at the end of the day. Everything she was going through seemed to point in one direction.

Self-diagnosis, however, had misled her a month earlier, and Carol feared her burning desire to bear a child was dictating her body's response a second time.

Each morning she pressed a hand over her stomach and whispered a fervent prayer that her weekend of lovemaking with Steve had found fertile ground. If she wasn't pregnant, then it would be April before they could try again, and that seemed like a thousand years away.

Carol was tempted to hurry out and buy another home pregnancy test. Then she would know almost immediately if her mind was playing tricks on her or if she really was pregnant. But she didn't. She couldn't explain — even to herself — why she was content to wait it out this time. If her monthly cycle was a week late, she decided, then and only then would she make an appointment with her doctor. But until that time she was determined to be strong — no matter what the test results said.

The one thing that astonished Carol the most was that in the time since Steve's deployment she missed him dreadfully. For months she'd done her utmost to drive every memory of that man from her mind, and sometimes she'd succeeded. Since Christmas, however, thoughts of Steve had dominated every waking minute. Until their weekend, Carol had assumed that was only natural. Steve Kyle did play a major role in her scheme to get pregnant. But she considered having a baby more of a bonus now. The possibility of rebuilding her marriage — which she had once considered impossible to do — claimed precedence.

Missing Steve wasn't a new experience. Carol had always felt at loose ends when he was aboard the *Atlantis*. But never had she felt quite like this. Nothing compared to the emotion that wrapped itself around her heart when she thought about Steve on this tour. She missed him so much that it frightened her. For more than a year she'd lived in the house alone; now it felt like an empty shell because he wasn't there. In bed at night her longing for him grew even more intense. She lay with her eyes closed, savoring the memory of their last two nights together. A chill washed over her at how close they'd come to destroying the love between them. The only thing that seemed to lessen this terrible longing she felt for her ex-husband was constructing dreams that involved him to help ease the loneliness as she drifted off to sleep.

Friday morning Carol woke feeling rotten and couldn't seem to force herself out of bed. She pulled into the huge Boeing parking lot at the Renton plant ten minutes later than usual and hurriedly locked her car. She was walking toward her building, trying to find the energy to rush when she heard someone call out her name.

She turned, but didn't see anyone she recognized.

"Carol, is that you?"

"Lindy?" Carol could hardly believe her eyes. It was Steve's sister. "What are you doing here?"

"I was just about to ask you the same thing."

Lindy looked fantastic. It had been nearly two years since Carol had last seen her former sister-in-law. Lindy had been a senior in college at the time, girlish and fun loving that summer she and Steve had visited his family. Had that been only two summers ago? It felt as though a decade had passed. Lindy had always held a special place in Carol's heart, and she smiled and hugged her close. When she drew back, Carol was surprised at the new maturity Lindy's eyes revealed.

"I work here," Lindy said, squeezing Carol's fingers. "I have since this past summer."

"Me, too — for over a year now."

Lindy tossed the sky a chagrined look. "You mean to tell me we've been employed by the same company, working at the same plant, and we didn't even know it?"

Carol laughed. "It looks that way."

They started walking toward the main entrance, still bemused, laughing and joking like long-lost sisters . . . which they were of sorts.

"I'm going to kick Steve," Lindy muttered. "He didn't tell me you worked for Boeing."

"He doesn't know. I suppose he assumes I'm still at Larson's Sporting Goods. I quit . . . long before the divorce was final. We haven't talked about my job, and I didn't think to mention it."

"How are you?" Lindy asked, but didn't give her more than a second to respond. "Steve growls at me every time I mention your name, which by the way, tells me he's still crazy about you."

Carol needed to hear that. She grinned, savoring the warm feeling Lindy's words gave her. "I'm still crazy about him, too."

"Oh, Carol," Lindy said with a giant sigh. "I can't tell you how glad I am to hear that. Steve never told any of us why the two of you divorced, but it nearly destroyed him. I can't tell you how happy I was when you phoned last Christmas. He hasn't been the same since."

"The divorce was wrong. . . . We should never have gone through with it," Carol said softly. Steve had been the one who had insisted on ending their marriage, and Carol had been too hurt, too confused to fight him the way she should have. Not wanting to linger on the mistakes of the past, Carol added, "Steve told me about you and Rush. Congratulations."

"Thanks." Lindy's eyes softened at the mention of Rush's name, and translucent joy radiated from her smile. "You met Paul didn't you?"

Carol nodded, recalling the time she had been introduced to Lindy's ex-fiancé in Minneapolis. She hadn't been overly impressed by him and, as she recalled, neither had Steve.

"He married . . . someone else," Lindy explained. "I was devastated, convinced my life was over. That's how I ended up in Seattle. I'm so happy I moved here. Paul did me the biggest favor of my life when he dumped me; I found Rush and we were meant to be together — we both know it."

Hold on to that feeling, Carol mused, saddened that she'd been foolish enough to allow Steve to walk away from her. It had been a mistake, and one they'd both paid for dearly. "I'm really pleased for you, Lindy," she said sincerely.

"Thank you . . . oh, Carol, I can't tell you how good it is to see you again."

They paused once they passed the security gate, delaying their parting. "What area are you working in?" Carol asked, stopping. The others flooding through the entrance gate walked a wide circle around them.

"Section B."

"F for me." Which meant they were headed in opposite directions.

"Perhaps we could meet for lunch one day," Lindy suggested, anxiously glancing at her watch.

"I'd like that. How about next Tuesday? I can't until then, I'm involved with a special project."

"Great. Call me. I'm on extension 314."

"Will do."

Steve walked past the captain's quarters and through the narrow hallway to his stateroom. Tired, he sat on the edge of his berth and rubbed his hand across his eyes. This was his favorite time of day. His shift was complete, and he had about an hour to kill before he thought about catching some sleep. For the past several days, he'd been writing Carol. His letter had become a journal of his thoughts. Chances were that he would be home long before the letter arrived. Because submarines spent their deployment submerged, there were few opportunities for the pickup or delivery of mail. Any emergencies were handled by radio transmission. There were occasions when they could receive mail, but it wasn't likely to happen this trip.

Steve felt good. From the moment his and Carol's divorce had been declared final, he'd felt as if he'd steered his life off course. He'd experienced the first turbulent storm and, instead of riding it out as he should have, he'd jumped overboard. Ever since, he'd felt out of sync with his inner self.

In his letter, he'd tried to explain that to Carol, but putting it in words had been as difficult as admitting it had been.

He didn't know what had happened between Todd and Carol. Frankly he didn't want to know. Whatever had been between them was over and Steve could have her back. Lord knew he wanted her. He was destined to go to his grave loving that woman.

When he'd sailed out of Hood Canal and into the Pacific Ocean, Steve had felt such an indescribable pull to the land. He loved his job, loved being a part of the Navy, but at that moment he would have surrendered his commission to have been able to stay in Seattle another month.

Although he'd told Carol that they should use this time apart to consider a reconciliation, he didn't need two seconds to know his own mind: he wanted them to remarry.

But first they had to talk, really talk, and not about Todd. There were some deep-rooted insecurities he'd faced the past couple of weeks that needed to be discussed.

One thing that had always bothered Steve was the fact that Carol had never seemed to need him. His peers continually related stories about how things fell apart at home while they were deployed. Upon their return, after the usual hugs and kisses, their wives handed them long lists of repairs needed around the house or relayed tales of horror they'd been left to deal with in their husband's absence.

Not Carol. She'd sent him off to sea, wearing a bright smile and greeted him with an identical one on his return. The impression she gave him was that it was great when he was home, but was equally pleasant if he wasn't.

Her easy acceptance of his life-style both pleased and irritated Steve. He appreciated the strength of her personality, and yet a small part of him wished she weren't quite so strong. He wasn't looking for a wife who was a clinging vine, but occasionally he wished for something less than Carol's sturdy oak-tree character. Just once he would have liked to hear her tell him how dreadful the weeks had been without him, or how she'd wished he'd been there to take care of the broken dryer or to change the oil in the car.

Instead she'd given him the impression that she'd been having a grand ol' time while he was at sea. She chatted about the classes she took, or how her herb garden was coming along. If he quizzed her about any problems, she brushed off his concern and assured him she'd already dealt with whatever turned up.

Steve knew Carol wasn't that involved in the Navy-wife activities. He figured it was up to her whether or not she joined. He hadn't pressed her, but he had wished she would make the effort to form friendships with the wives of his close friends.

Carol's apparent strength wasn't the only thing that troubled Steve, but it was one thing he felt they needed to discuss. The idea of telling his ex-wife that the least she could do was shed a few tears when he sailed away from her made him feel ungrateful. But swallowing his pride would be a small price to pay to straighten matters between them.

What she'd said about wanting a baby right away made him feel soft inside every time he thought about it. He'd yearned for them to start a family long before now, but Carol had always wanted to wait. Now she appeared eager. He didn't question her motivation. He was too damned grateful.

A knock on his door jerked his attention across the room. "Yes?"

Seaman Layle stepped forward. "The Captain would like to see you, sir."

Steve nodded and said, "I'll be right there."

Carol sat at the end of the examination table, holding a thin piece of tissue over her lap. The doctor would be in any minute to give her the news she'd been waiting to hear for the past month. Okay, so her period was two weeks late. There could be any number of reasons. For one thing, she'd been under a good deal of stress lately. For another . . .

Her thoughts came to a grinding halt as Dr.

Stewart stepped into the room. His glasses were perched on the end of his nose and his brow compressed as he read over her chart.

"Well?" she asked, unable to disguise the trembling eagerness in her voice.

"Congratulations, Carol," he said, looking up with a grandfatherly smile. "You're going to be a mother."

Chapter Seven

Carol was almost afraid to believe what Dr. Stewart was telling her; her hand flew to her heart. "You mean, I'm pregnant?"

The doctor looked up at her over the edge of his bifocals. "This is a surprise?"

"Oh, no . . . I knew — or at least I thought I knew." The joy that bubbled through her was unlike anything she had ever known. Ready tears blurred her vision and she bit her lower lip to hold back the tide that threatened to overwhelm her.

The doctor took her hand and gently patted it. "You're not sure how you feel — is that it?"

"Of course I do," she said, in a voice half an octave higher than usual. "I'm so happy I could just . . ."

"Cry?" he inserted.

"Dance," she amended. "This is the most wonderful thing that's ever happened to me since . . ."

"Your high-school prom?"

"Since I got married. I'm divorced now, but . . . Steve, he's my ex-husband, will marry me again . . . at least, I think he will. I'm not going to tell him about this right away. I don't want him to marry me again just because of the baby. I won't say a word about this. Or maybe I should? I don't know what to do, but thank you, Doctor, thank you so much."

A fresh smile began to form at the edges of his mouth. "You do whatever you think is best. Now, before we discuss anything else I want to go over some key points with you."

"Oh, of course, I'll do anything you say. I'll quit smoking and give up junk food, and take vitamins. If you really think it's necessary, I'll try to eat liver once a week."

His gaze reviewed her chart. "It says here you don't smoke."

"No, I don't, but I'd start just so I could quit if it would help the baby."

He chuckled. "I don't think that will be necessary, young lady."

Carol reached for his hand and pumped it several times. "I can't tell you how happy you've made me."

Still chuckling, the white-haired doctor said, "Tell me the same thing when you're in labor and I'll believe you."

Carol watched as Lindy entered the restaurant and paused to look around. Feeling a little self-conscious, she raised her hand. Lindy waved back and headed across the floor, weaving her way through the crowded tables.

"Hi. Sorry, I'm late."

"No problem." The extra time had given Carol a chance to study the menu. Her stomach had been so finicky lately that she had to be careful what she ate. This being pregnant was serious business and already the baby had made it clear "she" wasn't keen on particular foods — especially anything with tomatoes.

"Everything has been so hectic lately," Lindy said, picking up the menu, glancing at it and setting it aside almost immediately.

"That was quick," Carol commented, nodding her head toward the menu.

"I'm a woman who knows my own mind."

"Good for you," Carol said, swallowing a laugh. "What are you having?"

"I don't know. What are you ordering?"

"Soup and a sandwich," Carol answered, not fooled. Lindy wasn't interested in eating, she wanted answers. Steve's sister had been bursting with questions from the moment they'd met in the Boeing parking lot.

"Soup and a sandwich sounds good to me," Lindy said, obviously not wanting to waste time with idle chitchat.

Shaking her head, Carol studied Lindy. "Okay, go ahead and ask. I know you're dying to fire away."

Lindy unfolded the napkin and took pains spreading it over her lap. "Steve didn't come home Christmas Eve. . . . Well, he did, but it was early in the morning, and ever since that night he's been whistling 'Dixie.' " She paused and grinned. "Yet every time I said your name, he barked at me to mind my own business."

114

"We've seen each other since Christmas, too."

"You have?" Lindy pinched her lips together and sadly shook her head. "That brother of mine is so tight-lipped, I can't believe the two of us are related!"

Carol laughed. Unwittingly Lindy had pinpointed the crux of Carol and Steve's marital problems. They were each private people who preferred to keep problems inside rather than talking things out the way they should.

"So you've seen Steve since Christmas," Lindy prompted. "He must have contacted you after Rush and I moved."

"Actually I was the one who went to him."

"You did? Great."

"Yes," Carol nodded, blushing a little at the memory of how they'd spent that weekend. "It *was* great."

"Well, don't keep me in suspense here. Are you two going to get back together or what?"

"I think it's the 'or what.' "

"Oh." Lindy's gaze dropped abruptly and she frowned. "I don't mind telling you, I'm disappointed to hear that. I'd hoped you two would be able to work things out."

"We're heading in that direction, so don't despair. Steve and I are going to talk about a reconciliation when he returns."

"Oh, Carol, that's wonderful!"

"I think so, too."

"You two always seemed so right together.

The first time I saw Steve after you were divorced, I could hardly recognize him. He was so cynical and unhappy. He'd sit around the apartment and watch television for hours, or stare out the window."

"Steve did?" Carol couldn't imagine that. Steve always had so many things going — he'd never taken the time to relax when they were living together. Another problem had been that they didn't share enough of the same interests. Carol blamed herself for that, but she was willing to compromise now that her marriage was about to have new life breathed into it.

"I wasn't joking when I told you he's been miserable. I don't know what prompted you to contact him at Christmastime, but I thank God you did."

Carol smoothed her hand across her abdomen and smiled almost shyly. "I'm glad I did, too."

Steve's letter to Carol was nearly fifty pages in length now. The days, as they often did aboard a submarine, blended together. It felt as if they were six months into this cruise instead of two, but his eagerness to return to Carol explained a good deal of this interminable feeling.

Carol. His heart felt as though it would melt inside his chest every time he thought about her mentioning a baby. The first thing he was going to do after they'd talked was throw out her birth control pills. And then he was going to take her to bed and make slow, easy love to her.

Once he had her back, he wasn't going to risk losing her again.

In the past two months, Steve had made another decision. They needed to clear the air about Todd Larson. He'd promised her that he wouldn't mention the other man's name again, but he had to, just once, and then it would be finished. Laid to rest forever.

Finding Todd in their shower hadn't been the only thing that had led Steve to believe Carol and her employer were having an affair. There had been plenty of other clues. Steve just hadn't recognized them in the beginning.

For one, she'd been working a lot of overtime, and didn't seem to be getting paid for it. At first Steve hadn't given it much credence, although he'd been angry that often she couldn't see him off to sea properly. At the time, however, she'd seemed as sorry about it as he was.

His return home after a ten-week absence had been the real turning point. Until that tour, Carol had always been eager to make love after so many weeks apart. Normally they weren't in the house ten minutes before they found themselves in the bedroom. But not that time. Carol had greeted him with open arms, but she'd seemed reluctant to hurry to bed. He had gotten what he wanted, but fifteen minutes later she'd made some silly excuse about needing groceries and had left the house.

None of these events had made much sense at the time. Steve had suspected something might be wrong, but he hadn't known how to ask her, how to approach her without sounding like an insecure schoolboy. Soon afterward he'd flown east for a two-week communication class. It was when he'd arrived home unexpectedly early that he'd found Carol and Todd together.

The acid building up in his stomach seemed to explode with pain and Steve took in several deep breaths until the familiar ache passed. All these months he'd allowed Carol to believe he'd condemned her solely because he'd discovered another man in their home. It was more than that, much more, and it was time he freed his soul.

"Carol? Are you here?"

Carol remained sitting on the edge of the bathtub and pressed her hand over her forehead. "I'm in here." Her voice sounded weak and sick — which was exactly how she felt. The doctor had given her a prescription to help ease these dreadful bouts of morning sickness, but it didn't seem to be doing much good.

"Carol?" Once more Lindy's voice vibrated down the hallway and Carol heard the sound of approaching footsteps. "Carol, what's wrong? Should I call a doctor?"

"No . . . no, I'll be fine in a minute. My stomach has been a little queasy lately, is all."

"You look awful."

"I can't look any worse than I feel." Her feeble attempt at humor apparently didn't impress Lindy.

"I take it the sale at the Tacoma Mall doesn't interest you?"

"I tried to call," Carol explained, "but you'd already left. You go ahead without me."

"I'll do no such thing," Lindy answered vehemently. "You need someone to take care of you. When was the last time you had a decent meal?"

Carol pressed her hand over her stomach. "Please, don't even mention food."

"Sorry."

Lindy helped her back into a standing position and led her down the hallway to her bedroom. Carol was ashamed to have Steve's sister see the house when it looked as if a cyclone had gone through it, but she'd had so little energy lately. Getting to work and home again drained her. She went to bed almost immediately after dinner and woke up exhausted the next morning.

No one had told her being pregnant could be so demanding on her health. She'd never felt more sickly in her life. Her appointment with Dr. Stewart wasn't for another two weeks, but something had to be done. She couldn't go on like this much longer.

The April sun seemed to smile down on Steve as he stepped off the *Atlantis*. He paused and breathed in the glorious warmth of after-noon in the Pacific Northwest. Carol wouldn't be waiting for him, he knew. She had no way of knowing when he docked.

But she needn't come to him. He was going to her. The minute he got home, showered and shaved, he was driving over to her house. He was so ready for this.

They were going to talk, make love and get married. Maybe not quite that simply, but close.

He picked up his mail and let himself into the apartment. Standing beside the phone, he listened to the messages on his answering ma-chine. Three were from Lindy, who insisted he call first thing when he returned home.

He reached for the phone while he flipped through his assorted mail.

"You rang?" he asked cheerfully, when his sister answered.

"Steve? I'm so glad you called."

"What's wrong? Has Rush decided he's made a terrible mistake and decided to give you back to your dear, older brother to straighten out?" His sister didn't have an im-mediate comeback or a scathing reply, which surprised him.

"Steve, it's Carol."

His blood ran cold with fear. "What hap-pened?"

"I don't know, but I wanted to talk to you be-fore you went to see her," she said and hesitated. "You were planning on going there right away, weren't you?"

"Yes. Now tell me what's the matter with Carol."

"She's been sick."

"How sick?" His heart was thundering against his chest with worry.

"I . . . don't think it's anything . . . serious, but I thought I should warn you before you surprise her with a visit. She's lost weight and looks terrible, and she'll never forgive you if you show up without warning her you're in town."

"Has she seen a doctor?"

"I . . . don't know," Lindy confessed. "She won't talk about it."

"What the hell could be wrong?"

The line seemed to vibrate with electricity. "If you want the truth, I suspect she's pregnant."

Chapter Eight

"Pregnant?" Steve repeated and the word boomeranged against the walls of his mind with such force that the mail he'd been sorting slipped from his fingers and fell to the floor. He said it again. "Pregnant. But . . . but . . ."

"I probably shouldn't have said anything." Lindy's soft voice relayed her confusion. "But honestly, Steve, I've been so worried about her. She looks green around the gills and she's much too thin to be losing so much weight. I told her she should see a doctor, but she just smiles and says there's nothing to worry about."

The wheels in Steve's mind were spinning fast. "The best thing I can do is talk to her, and find out what's happening."

"Do that, but for heaven's sake be gentle with her. She's too fragile for you to come at her like Hulk Hogan."

"I wouldn't do that."

"Steve, I'm your sister. I know you!"

"Okay, okay. I'll talk to you later." He hung up the phone but kept his hand on the receiver while he mulled over his sister's news. Carol had said she wanted to have a baby, and she knew how he felt about the subject.

He'd longed for a family since the first year they were together.

However, they weren't married now. No problem. Getting remarried was a minor detail. All he had to do was talk to the chaplain and make the arrangements. And if what Lindy said was true, the sooner he saw the chaplain, the better.

Without forethought he jerked the receiver off the hook and jabbed out Carol's number with his index finger. After two rings, he decided this kind of discussion was better done in person.

He showered, changed clothes and was halfway out the door when he remembered what Lindy had said about letting Carol know he was coming. Good idea.

He marched back over to the phone and dialed her number one more time.

No answer.

"Damn." He started pacing the floor, feeling restless, excited and nervous. He couldn't stay in the apartment; the walls felt as if they were closing in on him. He'd spent the last three months buried in the belly of a nuclear submarine and hadn't experienced a twinge of claustrophobia. Twenty minutes inside his apartment, knowing what he now did, and he was going ape.

He had to get out there even if it meant parking outside Carol's house and waiting for her to return.

He rushed out to his car and was grateful when it started right away after sitting for three months.

He was going to be a father! His heart swelled with joy and he experienced such a sense of elation that he wanted to throw back his head and shout loud enough to bring down brick walls.

A baby. His and Carol's baby. His throat thickened with emotion, and he had to swallow several times to keep from breaking down and weeping right there on the freeway. A new life. They were going to bring a tiny little being into this world and be accountable for every aspect of the infant's life. The responsibility seemed awesome. His hands gripped the steering wheel and he sucked in a huge breath as he battled down his excitement and fears.

He was going to be a good father. Always loving and patient. Everything would be right for his son . . . or daughter. Male chauvinist that he was, he yearned for a son. They could have a daughter the second time, but the thought of Carol giving him a boy felt right in his mind.

But he had so much to learn, so much to take care of. First things first. Steve tried to marshal his disjointed thoughts. He had to see to Carol's health. If this pregnancy was as hard on her as Lindy implied, then he wanted Carol to quit her job. He made good money; she should stay home and build up her strength.

The drive to Carol's house took less than fifteen minutes, and when Steve pulled up and parked he noticed her car in the driveway with the passenger door opened. His heart felt like it was doing jumping jacks, he was so eager to see her.

The front door opened and Carol stepped outside and to her car, grabbing a bag of groceries.

"Carol." She hadn't seen him.

She turned abruptly at the sound of her name. "Steve," she cried out brokenly and dropped the brown shopping bag. Without the least bit of hesitation, she came flying across the lawn.

He met her halfway, and wrapping his arms around her waist, he closed his eyes to the welcome feel of her body against his. His happiness couldn't be contained and he swung her around. Her lips were all over his face, kissing him, loving him, welcoming him.

Steve drank in her love and it humbled him. He held her gently, fearing he would hurt her, and kissed her with an aching tenderness, his mouth playing over the dewy softness of hers.

His hands captured her face and her deep blue eyes filled with tears as she smiled tremulously at him. "I've missed you so much. These have been the longest three months of my life."

"Mine, too." His voice nearly choked, and he kissed her again in an effort to hide the tide of emotion he was experiencing.

Steve picked up the scattered groceries for her and they walked into the house together.

"Go ahead and put those in the kitchen. Are you hungry?"

She seemed nervous and flittered from one side of the room to the other.

"I could fix you something if you'd like," she suggested, her back braced against the kitchen counter.

Steve's eyes held hers, and the emotion that had rocked him earlier built with intensity every minute he was in her presence. "You know what I want," he whispered, hardly able to speak.

Carol relaxed, and blushed a little. "I want to make love with you so much."

He held his hands out to her and she walked toward him, locking her arms around his neck. She pressed her weight against him and Steve realized how slender she was, how fragile. Regret slammed into his chest with all the force of a wrecking ball against a concrete wall. She was nurturing his child within her womb, for God's sake, and all he could think about was getting her into bed. He hadn't even asked her how she was feeling. All he cared about was satisfying his own selfish lusts.

"Carol . . ." His breath was slow and labored. Gently he tried to break free, because he couldn't think straight when she was touching him.

"Hmm?" Her hands were already working at

his belt buckle, and her mouth was equally busy.

He felt himself weakening. "Are you sure? I mean, if you'd rather not . . ."

She released his zipper and when her hands closed around his naked hardness, he thought he would faint. His eyes rolled toward the ceiling. "Don't . . . don't you think we should talk?" he managed to say.

"No."

"But —"

She broke away and looked up at him, her eyes hungry with demand. "Steven Kyle, what is your problem? Do you or do you not want to make love?"

"I think . . . we should probably talk first. Don't you?" He didn't know if she would take him seriously with his voice shaking the way it was.

She grinned, and when her gaze dropped to below his waistline, they rounded. "No. Because neither one of us is going to be able to say anything worth listening to until we take care of other things. . . ."

It wasn't possible to love a woman any more than he did Carol at that moment, Steve thought. She reached for his hand and led him out of the kitchen and into the bedroom.

Like a lost sheep, he followed.

The newborn moon cast silvery shadows on the wall opposite the bed, and Steve sighed, feeling sated and utterly content. Carol slept at his side, her arm draped around his middle and her face nestled against his shoulder. Her tousled hair fell over his chest and he ran his fingers through it, letting the short, silky length slip through his hands.

Gently he brushed a blond curl off her cheek and twisted his head so that he could kiss her temple. She stirred and sighed in her sleep. He grinned. If he searched for a hundred years he would never find a woman who could satisfy him the way Carol did.

They hadn't talked, hadn't done anything but make love until they were both so exhausted that sleep dominated their minds. They may not have voiced the words, but the love between them was so secure it would take more than a bulldozer to rock it this time. Steve may not have had a chance to say the words, but his heart had been speaking them from the minute Carol had led him to bed.

Bringing the blanket more securely over her shoulders, he wrapped his arm around her and studied her profile in the fading moonlight. What Lindy told him was true. Carol had lost weight; she was as slender as a bamboo shoot, and much too pale. She needed someone to take care of her and, he vowed in his heart, he would be the one.

He almost wished she would roll over so that he could place his hand on her abdomen and feel for himself the life that was blossoming there. He felt weak with happiness every time he thought about their baby. He closed his eyes at the sudden longing that seared through his blood.

Carol hadn't yet told him that she was pregnant but he was sure she would in the morning. Until then, he would be content.

He closed his eyes and decided to sleep.

Steve woke first. Carol didn't so much as stir when he climbed out of bed and reached for his clothes. Silently he tiptoed out of the room and gently closed the door. She needed her sleep.

He made himself a pot of coffee and piddled around the kitchen, putting away the groceries that had been sitting on the counter all night. He pulled open the vegetable bin and carelessly tossed a head of lettuce in there. The drawer refused to close and he discovered the problem to be a huge shriveled up sweet potato. He took it out and, with an over the head loop shot Michael Jordan would have envied, tossed it into the garbage.

Carol and sweet potatoes. Honestly. The last time he'd looked inside her refrigerator, it had been filled with the stuff in every imaginable form.

He supposed he should get used to that kind of thing. It was a well-known fact that women often experienced weird food cravings when they were pregnant. Sweet potatoes were only one step above pickles and ice cream.

Just a minute! That had been last Christmas
. . . before Christmas.

Steve's heart seemed to stop and slowly he
straightened. Chewing on the inside of his lip,
he closed the refrigerator door. Carol had been
stuffing down the sweet potatoes long before
he'd accepted her dinner invitation. Weeks before, from the look of it.

His thoughts in chaos, he stumbled into the
living room and slumped into the chair. An icy
chill settled over him. No. He refused to believe
it, refused to condemn her on anything so
flimsy. Then his gaze fell on a pair of knitting
needles. He reached for her pattern book and
noted the many designs for infant wear.

His heart froze. The last time he'd been by
the house, Carol had been knitting a baby
blanket. When he'd asked her about it, she'd
told him it was for a friend. His snort of
laughter was mirthless. Sure, Carol! More lies,
more deceit.

And come to think of it, on Christmas Eve
she'd pushed her knitting aside so that he
couldn't see it. She'd been knitting the *same*
blanket for the *same* friend then, too.

He was still stewing when Carol appeared.
She smiled at him so sweetly as she slipped her
arms into her robe.

"Morning," she said with a yawn.

"Morning."

His gruffness must have stopped her. "Is
something wrong?"

Such innocent eyes . . . She'd always been able to fool him with that look. No more.

"Steve?"

"You're pregnant, aren't you?"

She released her breath in a long, slow sigh. "I wondered if you'd guess. I suppose I should have told you right away, but . . . we got side-tracked, didn't we?"

He could hardly stand to look at her.

"You're not angry, are you?" she asked, her eyes suddenly reflecting uncertainty.

Again such innocence, such skill. "No, I suppose not."

"Oh, good," she said with a feeble smile, "you had me worried there for a minute."

"One question?"

"Sure."

"Just whose baby is it?"

Chapter Nine

"Whose baby is it?" Carol repeated, stunned. She couldn't believe Steve would dare to ask such a question when the answer was so obvious.

"That's what I want to know."

His face was drawn extremely tight — almost menacing. She moved into the room and sat across from him, her heart ready to explode with dread. She met his look squarely, asking no quarter, giving none. The prolonged moment magnified the silence.

"I'm three months pregnant. This child is yours," she said, struggling to keep her voice even.

"Don't lie to me, Carol. I'm not completely dense." The anger that seeped into his expression was fierce enough to frighten her. Steve vaulted to his feet and started pacing in military fashion, each step precise and clipped, as if the drill would put order to his thoughts and ultimately to his life.

Carol's fingernails dug into the fabric on the sides of the overstuffed chair and her pulse went crazy. Her expression, however, revealed none of the inner turmoil she was experiencing. When her throat felt as if it would cooperate with her tongue, she spoke. "How can you even think such a thing?"

Steve splayed his fingers and jerked them through his hair in an action that seemed savage enough to yank it out by the roots. "I should have known something was wrong when you first contacted me at Christmastime."

Carol felt some color flush into her cheeks; to her regret it probably convinced Steve she was as guilty as he believed.

"That excuse about not wanting to spend Christmas alone was damn convenient. And if that wasn't obvious enough, your little seduction scene should have been. God knows, I fell for it." He whirled around to face her. "You did plan that, didn't you?"

"I . . . I . . ."

"Didn't you?" he repeated, in harsh tones that demanded the truth.

Miserable and confused, Carol nodded. She had no choice but to admit to her scheme of seducing him.

One corner of his mouth curved up in a half smile, but there was no humor or amusement in the action. The love that had so recently shone from his eyes had been replaced by condemnation.

"If only you would let me explain." She tried again, shocked by this abrupt turn of events. Only a few hours before, they'd lain in each other's arms and spoken of a reconciliation. The promise that had sprung to life between them was wilting and she was powerless to stop it.

"What could you possibly say that would

change the facts?" he demanded. "I was always a fool when it came to you. Even after a year apart I hadn't completely come to terms with the divorce and you, no doubt, knew that and used it to your advantage."

"Steve, I —"

"It's little wonder," he continued, not allowing her to finish speaking, "that you considered me that perfect patsy for this intrigue. You used my love for you against me."

"Okay, so I planned our lovemaking Christmas Eve. You're right about that. I suppose I was pretty obvious about the whole thing when you think about it. But I had a reason. A damn good one."

"Yes, I know."

Carol hadn't realized a man's eyes could be so cold.

"What do you know?" she asked.

"That cake you're baking in your oven isn't mine."

"Oh, honestly, Steve. Your paranoia is beginning to wear a little thin. I'm doing my damnedest to keep my cool here, but you're crazy if you think anyone else could be the father."

He raised his index finger. "You're good. You know that? You're really very good. That fervent look about you, as though I'm going off the deep end to even suspect you of such a hideous deed. Just the right amount of indignation while keeping your anger in check. Good, very good."

"Stop that," she shouted. "You're being ridiculous. When you get in this mood, nothing appeases you. Everything I say becomes suspect."

His hand wiped his face free of expression. "If I didn't know better, I could almost believe you."

She hated it when Steve was like this. He was so convinced he was right that no amount of arguing would ever persuade him otherwise. "I'm going to tell you one last time, and then I won't say it again. Not ever. We — as in you and I, Steve — are going to have a baby."

Steve stared at her for so long that she wasn't sure what he was thinking. He longed to believe her — she could recognize that yearning in his eyes — and yet something held him back. His Adam's apple moved up and down, and he clenched his jaw so tightly that the sides of his face went white. Still the inner struggle continued while he glared at her, as if commanding the truth — as if to say he could deal with anything as long as it was true.

Carol met that look, holding her gaze as steady and sure as was humanly possible. He wanted the truth, and she'd already given it to him. Nothing she could say would alter the facts: he was her baby's father.

Steve then turned his back on her. "The problem is, I desperately want to believe you. I'd give everything I've managed to accumulate in this life to know that baby was mine."

Everything about Steve, the way he stood

with his shoulders hunched, his feet braced as if he expected a blow, told Carol he didn't believe her. Her integrity was suspect.

"I . . . my birthday — I was thirty," she said, faltering as she scrambled to make him recognize the truth. "It hit me then that my childbearing years were numbered. Since the divorce I've been so lonely, so unhappy, and I thought a baby would help fill the void in my life."

He turned to look at her as she spoke, then closed his eyes and nodded.

Just looking at the anguish in his face was almost more than Carol could bear. "I know you never believed me about Todd, but there's only been one lover in my life, and that's you. I figured that you owed me a baby. I thought if I invited you to spend Christmas with me and you accepted, that I could probably steer us into the bedroom. None of the problems we had in our marriage had extended there."

"Carol, don't — this isn't necessary. I already know you were —"

"Yes, it is. Please, Steve, you've got to listen to me. You've got to understand."

He turned away from her again, but Carol continued talking because it was the only thing left for her to do. If she didn't tell him now, there might never be another chance.

"I didn't count on anything more happening between us. I'd convinced myself I was emotionally separated from you by that time and all I needed was the baby . . ."

"You must have been worried when I didn't fall into your scheme immediately."

"What do you mean?" Carol felt frantic and helpless.

"I didn't immediately suggest we get back together — that must have had you worried. After Christmas Eve we decided to leave things as they were." He walked away from her, but not before she saw the tilt of righteous indignation in his profile. "That visit to my apartment . . . what was your excuse? Ah yes, a button you'd found and thought might be mine. Come on, Carol, you should have been more original than that. As excuses go, that's about as flimsy as they get."

"All right, if you want me to admit I planned that seduction scene, too, then I will. I didn't get pregnant the way I planned in December . . . I had to try again. You had to know swallowing my pride and coming to you wasn't easy."

He nodded. "No, I don't suppose it was."

"Then you believe me?"

"No."

Carol hung her head in frustration.

"Naturally only one night of lovemaking wasn't enough," he said with a soft denunciation. "It made sense to plan more than one evening together in case I started questioning matters later. I'm pleased that you did credit me with some intelligence. Turning up pregnant after one time together would have seemed much too convenient. But twice . . . Well, that sounds far more likely."

Carol was speechless. Once more Steve had tried and found her guilty, choosing to believe the worst possible scenario.

"Fool that I am, I should have known something was up by how docile and loving you were. So willing to forget the past, forgive and go on with the future. Then there was all that talk about us starting a family. That sucked me right in, didn't it? You know, you've always known how much I want children."

"There's nothing I can say, is there?"

"No," he admitted bleakly. "I wonder what you would have told me next summer when you gave birth — although months premature, astonishingly the baby would weigh six or seven pounds and obviously be full term. Don't you think I would have questioned you then?"

She kept her mouth shut, refusing to be drawn into this kind of degrading verbal battle. From experience she knew nothing she could say would vindicate her.

"If you don't want to claim this child, Steve, that's fine, the loss is yours. My original intent was to raise her alone anyway. I'd thought . . . I'd hoped we could build a new life together, but it's obvious I was wrong."

"Dead wrong. I won't let you make a fool of me a second time."

A strained moment passed before Carol spoke, and when she did her voice was incred-

138

ibly weak. "I think it would be best if you left now."

He answered her with an abrupt nod, turned away and went to her bedroom to retrieve his shirt and shoes.

Carol didn't follow him. She sat, feeling numb and growing more ill with each minute. The nausea swelled up inside her until she knew she was going to empty her stomach. Standing, she rushed into the bathroom and leaned over the toilet in a ritual that had become all too familiar.

When she'd finished, she discovered Steve waiting in the doorway, watching her. She didn't know how long he'd been there.

"Are you all right?"

She nodded, not looking at him, wanting him to leave so that she could curl into a tight ball and lick her wounds. No one could hurt her the way Steve did. No other man possessed the power.

He didn't seem to believe she was going to be fine, and slowly he came into the bathroom. He wet a washcloth and handed it to her, waiting while she wiped her face. Then, gently, he led her back into the bedroom and to the bed. Carol discovered that lying down did seem to ease the dizzy, sick feeling.

Steve took his own sweet time buttoning his shirt, apparently stalling so that he could stick by her in case she was sick a second time, although she knew he would never have admitted he cared. If she'd had the energy, Carol would have suggested he go, because for every minute he lingered it was more difficult for her to bear seeing him. She didn't want him to care about her — how could he when he believed the things he did? And yet, every now and again she would find him watching her guardedly, his eyes filled with worry.

"When do you see the doctor next?" He walked around the foot of the bed and resumed an alleged search for his socks.

"Two weeks." Her voice was faint and barely audible.

"Don't you think you should give him a call sooner?"

"No." She refused to look at him.

Steve apparently found what he wanted. He sat on the edge of the mattress and slowly, methodically put on his shoes. "How often does this sort of thing happen?" he asked next.

"It doesn't matter." Some of her energy returned, and she tested her strength by sitting up. "Listen, Steve, I appreciate your concern, but it just isn't necessary. My baby and I are going to be just fine."

He didn't look convinced. His brooding gaze revealed his thoughts, and when he looked at her, his expression softened perceptibly. It took a moment for his eyes to drop to her hand, which rested on her abdomen.

The change that came over him was a shock. His face tightened and his mouth thinned. A surge of anger shot through her. "You don't want to claim our daughter, then it's your loss."

"The baby isn't mine."

The anguish in his voice was nearly Carol's undoing. She bit her lower lip and shook her head with mounting despair. "I can't believe you're actually saying that. But you'll never know, will you, Steve? All your life you're going to be left wondering. If she has dark eyes like yours and dark hair, that will only complicate your doubts. No doubt the Kyle nose will make you all the more suspicious. Someday you're going to have to face the fact that you've rejected your own child. If you can live with that, then so be it."

He twisted around and his fists were knotted into tight fists. "You were pregnant at Christmas and you're trying to pawn this pregnancy off on me."

"That is the most insulting thing you've ever said to me."

He didn't answer her for a long time. "You've insulted my intelligence. I may have loved you, but I'm not a blind fool."

"They don't come any blinder."

"Explain the milk?"

"What?" Carol hadn't a clue to what he was talking about.

"At Christmas, after we'd made love, we had a snack. Remember?"

Carol did.

"You poured yourself a glass of milk and I

commented because you used to dislike it. We were married five years and the only time I can remember you having milk was with cold cereal. You could live your whole life without the stuff. All of a sudden you're drinking it by the glassful."

With deliberate calm Carol rolled her gaze toward the ceiling. "Talk about flimsy excuses. You honestly mean to say you're rejecting your own child because I drank a glass of milk an entire month before I was pregnant?"

"That isn't everything. I saw your knitting Christmas Eve, although you tried to hide it from me. Later, I asked you about it and you claimed it was a baby blanket. It was the same piece you were working on at Christmas, wasn't it?"

"Yes, but . . ."

"That blanket's for your baby isn't it, Carol? There never was any friend."

Frustration mounting in volcanic proportions, she yelled, "All right, it wasn't for any friend — that's what you want to hear."

"And then there were the sweet potatoes. Good God, you had six containers full of yams that night . . . pregnant women are said to experience silly cravings. And that's what it was, wasn't it — a craving?"

Standing, Carol felt the weight of defeat settle on her shoulders. No amount of arguing would change anything now. Steve had reasoned everything out in his own mind and found her answers lacking. There was no argument she could give him that would change what he'd already decided.

"Well?" he demanded. "Explain those things away, if you can."

She felt as if she were going to burst into helpless tears at any second. For six years she'd loved this man and given him the power to shatter her heart. "You're the only man I know who can put two and two together and come up with five, Steve," she said wearily.

"For God's sake, quit lying. Quit trying to make me doubt what's right before my eyes. You wanted to trick me into believing that baby is mine, and by God, it almost worked."

If he didn't leave soon, Carol was going to throw him out. "I think you should leave."

"Admit it!" he shouted.

Nothing less would satisfy him. She slapped her hands against her thighs and feigned a sorrowful sigh. "I guess you're just too smart for me. I should have known better than to try to fool you."

Steve turned and marched to the front door, but stopped, his hand gripping the knob. "What's he going to do about it?"

"Who?"

"Todd."

It took every dictate of Carol's control not to scream that her former employer had nothing to do with her being pregnant. "I don't have anything more to say to you."

"Is he going to divorce Joyce and marry you?"

With one hand cradled around her middle, Carol pointed to the door with the other.

"I have a right to know," Steve argued. "If he isn't going to help you, something should be done."

"I don't need anything — especially from you."

"As much as I'd like to walk away from you, I can't. If you find yourself in trouble, call me. I'll always be there for you."

"If you want to help me, then get out of my life. This baby is mine and mine alone." There was no anger in her words; her voice was low and controlled . . . and sad, unbelievably sad.

Steve hesitated and his lingering seemed to imply that something would change. Carol knew otherwise.

"Goodbye, Steve."

He paused, then whispered, "Goodbye."

The pain in his voice would haunt her all her days, she thought, as Steve turned and walked out of her life.

The loud pounding noise disrupted Steve's restless slumber and he sat up and glared at the front door of his apartment.

"Who is it?" he shouted, and the sound of his own voice sent shooting pains through his temple. He moaned, tried to sit up and in the process nearly fell off the sofa.

"Steve, I know you're in there. Open up."

Lindy. Damn, he should have known it would be his meddling sister. He wished to hell she would just leave him alone. He'd managed to put her off for the past week, avoiding talking to her, inventing excuses not to see her. Obviously that hadn't been good enough because here she was!

"Go away," he said, his voice less loud this time. "I'm sick." That at least was the truth. His head felt like someone had used it for batting practice.

"I have my own key and I'll use it unless you open this door right now."

Muttering under his breath, Steve weaved across the floor until he reached the door. The carpet seemed to pitch and roll like a ship tossed about in a storm. He unbolted the lock and stepped aside so Lindy could let herself in. He knew she was about to parade into his apartment like an angel of mercy prepared to save him from hell and damnation.

He was right.

Lindy came into the room with the flourish of a suffragette marching for equality of the sexes. She stopped in the middle of the room, hands placed righteously on her hips, and studied him as though viewing the lowest form of human life. Then slowly she began to shake her head with obvious disdain.

"You look like hell," she announced.

Steve almost expected bugles to follow her

decree. "Thank you, Mother Teresa."

"Sit down before you fall down."

Steve did as she ordered simply because he didn't have the energy to argue. "Would you mind not talking so loud?"

With one hand remaining on her hip, Lindy marched over to the window and pulled open the drapes.

Steve squinted under the force of the sunlight and shaded his eyes. "Was that really necessary?"

"Yes." She walked over to the coffee table and picked up an empty whiskey bottle, as though by touching it she was exposing herself to an incurable virus. With her nose pointed toward the ceiling, she walked into the kitchen and tossed it in the garbage. The bottle made a clanking sound as it hit against other bottles.

"How long do you intend to keep yourself holed up like this?" she demanded.

He shrugged. "As long as it takes."

"Steve, for heaven's sake be reasonable."

"Why?"

She couldn't seem to find an answer and that pleased him because he wasn't up to arguing with her. He knew there was a reason to get up, get dressed and eat, but he hadn't figured out what it was yet. He'd taken a week of leave in order to spend time with Carol. Now he would give anything to have to report to duty — anything to take his mind off his ex-wife.

His mouth felt like a sand dune had shifted

146

there while he slept. He needed something cold and wet. With Lindy following him, he walked into the kitchen and got himself a beer.

To his utter amazement, his sister jerked it out of his hand and returned it to the refrigerator. "From the look of things, I'd say you've had enough to drink."

He was so stunned, he didn't know what to say.

She pointed her index finger toward a kitchen chair, silently ordering him to sit. From the determined look she wore, Steve decided not to test her.

Before he could object, she had a pot of coffee brewing and was rummaging through the refrigerator looking for God knew what. Eggs, he realized when she brought out a carton.

She insisted he eat, which he did, but he didn't like it. While he sat at the table like an obedient child, Lindy methodically started emptying his sink, which was piled faucet-high with dirty dishes.

"You don't need to do that," he objected.

"Yes, I know."

"Then don't . . . I can get by without any favors from you." Now that he had something in his stomach, he wasn't about to be led around like a bull with a ring through his nose.

"You need something," she countered. "I'm just not sure what. I suspect it's a swift kick in the seat of the pants."

"You and what army, little sister."

Lindy declined to answer. She poured herself a cup of coffee, replenished his and claimed the chair across the table from him. "Okay," she said, her shoulders rising with an elongated sigh. "What happened with Carol?"

At the mention of his former wife's name, Steve's stomach clenched in a painful knot. Just thinking about her carrying another man's child produced such an inner agony that the oxygen constricted his lungs and he couldn't breathe.

"Steve?"

"Nothing happened between us. Absolutely nothing."

"Don't give me that. The last time we talked, you were as excited as a puppy about her being pregnant. You could hardly wait to see her. What's happened since then?"

"I already told you — nothing!"

Lindy slumped forward and braced her hand against her forehead. "You've buried yourself in this apartment for an entire week and you honestly expect me to believe that?"

"I don't care what you believe."

"I'm to blame, aren't I?"

"What?"

"I shouldn't have said a word about Carol and the baby, but she'd been so sick and I've been so concerned about her." Lindy paused and lightly shook her head. "I still am."

Steve hated the way his heart reacted to the news that Carol was still sickly. He didn't want to care about her, didn't want to feel this instant surge of protectiveness when it came to his ex-wife. For the past week, he'd tried to erase every memory of her from his tortured mind. Obviously it hadn't worked, and the only thing he'd managed to develop was one hell of a hangover.

"I shouldn't have told you," Lindy repeated.

"It wouldn't have made one bit of difference; I would have found out sooner or later."

Lindy's hands cupped the coffee mug. "What are you going to do about it?"

Steve shrugged. "Nothing."

"Nothing? But Steve, that's your baby."

He let that pass, preferring not to correct his sister. "What's between Carol and me isn't any of your business. Leave it at that."

She seemed to weigh his words carefully. "I wish I could."

"What do you mean by that?"

"Carol looks awful. I really think she needs to see her doctor. Something's wrong, Steve. She shouldn't be this sick."

He shrugged with feigned indifference. "That's her problem."

Lindy's jaw sagged open. "I can't believe you. Carol is carrying your child and you're acting like she got pregnant all by herself."

Steve diverted his gaze to the blue sky outside his living-room window and shrugged. "Maybe she did," he whispered.

Chapter Ten

Carol sat at her desk and tried to concentrate on her work. This past seven days had been impossible. Steve honestly believed she was carrying another man's child, and nothing she could ever say would convince him otherwise. It was like history repeating itself and all the agony of her divorce had come back to haunt her.

Only this time Carol was smarter.

If Steve chose to believe such nonsense, that was his problem. She wanted this baby and from the first had been prepared to raise her daughter alone. Now if only she could get over these bouts of nausea and the sickly feeling that was with her almost every day and night. Most of it she attributed to the emotional upheaval in her life. Within a couple of weeks it would pass and she would feel a thousand times better — at least, that was what she kept telling herself.

"Hi."

A familiar, friendly voice invaded Carol's thoughts. "Lindy!" she said, directing her attention to Steve's sister. "What are you doing here?"

"Risking my job and my neck. Can we meet later? I've got to talk to you; it's important."

As fond as Carol was of her former sister-in-law, she knew there was only one subject Lindy would want to discuss, and that was Steve. Her former husband was a topic Carol preferred to avoid. Nor was she willing to justify herself to his sister, if Lindy started questioning her about the baby's father. It would be better for everyone involved if she refused to meet her, but the desperate worry in Lindy's steady gaze frightened her.

"I suppose you want to ask me about Steve," Carol said slowly, thoughtfully. "I don't know that any amount of talking is going to change things. It'd be best just to leave things as they are."

"Not you, too."

"Too?"

"Steve's so closed mouthed you'd think your name was listed as classified information."

Carol picked up the clipboard and flipped over a page, in an effort to pretend she was exceptionally busy. "Maybe it's better this way," she murmured, but was unable to disguise the pain her words revealed.

"Listen, I've got to get back before someone important — like my supervisor — notices I'm missing," Lindy said, scribbling something on a pad and ripping off the sheet. "Here's the address to my apartment. Rush is on sea trials, so we'll be alone."

"Lindy . . ."

"If you care anything about my brother you'll come." Once more those piercing eyes spelled out his sister's concern.

Carol took the address, and frowned. "Let me tell you right now that if you're trying to orchestrate a reconciliation, neither one of us will appreciate it."

"I . . ."

"Is Steve going to mysteriously arrive around the same time as I do?"

"No. I promise he won't. Good grief, Carol, he won't even talk to me anymore. He isn't talking to anyone. I'm not kidding when I say I'm worried about him."

Carol soaked in that information and frowned, growing concerned herself.

"You'll come?"

Against her better judgment, she nodded. Like her ex-husband, she didn't want to talk to anyone, and especially not to someone related to Steve. The pain of his accusations was still too raw to share with someone else.

Yet she knew she would be there to talk about whatever it was Lindy found so important, although she also knew that nothing Lindy could say would alter her relationship with Steve.

At five-thirty, Carol parked her car outside Lindy's apartment building. She regretted agreeing to the meeting, but couldn't see any way of escaping without going back on her word.

Lindy opened the door and greeted her with a weak smile. "Come in and sit down. Would you like something cold to drink? I just finished making a pitcher of iced tea."

"That sounds fine." Carol still wasn't feeling well and would be glad when she saw her doctor for her regular appointment. She took a seat in the living room while Lindy disappeared into the kitchen.

Lindy returned a couple of minutes later with tall glasses filled with iced tea.

"I wish I could say you're looking better," Lindy said, handing Carol a glass and a colorful napkin.

"I wish I could say I was, too."

Lindy sat across from her and automatically crossed her long legs. "I take it the medication the doctor gave you for the nausea didn't help?"

"It helped some."

"But generally you're feeling all right?"

Carol shrugged. She'd never been pregnant before and had nothing to compare this experience to. "I suppose."

Lindy's fingers wiped away the condensation on the outside of her glass. She hedged, and her gaze drifted around the room. "I think the best way to start is to apologize."

"But what could you have possibly done to offend me?"

Lindy's gaze moved to Carol's, and she released a slow breath. "I told Steve I suspected you were pregnant."

"It's true," Carol answered with a gentle

smile. She would be a single mother, and although she would have preferred to be married, she was pleased and proud to be carrying this child.

"I know . . . but it would have been far better coming from you. I left a message for Steve to call me once he returned from his deployment. I was afraid he was going to come at you with his usual caveman tactics and you've been so ill lately . . . It's a weak excuse, I know."

"Lindy, for goodness' sake, don't worry about it. This baby isn't a deep, dark secret." Remembering the life she was nurturing in her womb was what had gotten her through the bleakest hours of this past week. Steve might choose to reject his daughter, but he could never take away this precious gift he had unknowingly given her.

"I don't know what's going on with my brother," Lindy muttered, dropping her gaze to her tea. "I wish Rush were here. If anyone could talk some sense into him, it's my husband."

"Get used to him being away when you need him most. It's the lot of a Navy wife. The Navy blues doesn't always refer only to their dress uniform, you know."

Lindy nodded. "I'm learning that; I'm also learning I'm much stronger than I thought I was. Rush was involved in an accident last year in the Persian Gulf — you probably read about it in the papers — well, really that doesn't have anything to do with Steve, but he was with me the whole time when we didn't know if Rush was dead or alive. I can't even begin to tell you how good he was, how supportive. In a crisis, my brother can be a real trooper."

"Yes, I know." Carol paused and took a sip of her tea. On more than one occasion in their married life, she had come to admire Steve's levelheadedness in dealing with both major and minor emergencies. It was in other matters, like trust and confidence in her love, that he fell sadly short.

"I don't understand him anymore," Lindy admitted. "He was ecstatic when I mentioned my suspicions about you being pregnant . . . I thought he was going to go right through the ceiling he was so excited. He was bubbling over like a little kid. I know he drove over to your place right after that and then we didn't hear from him again. I phoned, but he just barked at me to leave him alone, and when I went to see him . . . well, that's another story entirely."

Carol stiffened. It was better to deal with Lindy honestly since it was apparent Steve hadn't told her. "He doesn't believe the baby is his."

Lindy's brow folded into a dark, brooding frown. "But that's ridiculous."

Carol found it somewhat amazing that her former sister-in-law would believe her without question and her ex-husband wouldn't.

"I . . . can't believe this." Lindy pressed her

palm over her forehead, lifting her bangs, and her mouth sagged open. "But, sadly, it explains a good deal." As if she couldn't remain sitting any longer, Lindy got up and started walking around the room, moving from one side to the other without direction. "What is that man's problem? Good grief, someone should get him to face a few fundamental facts here."

Carol smiled. It felt good to have someone trust and believe her.

"What are you going to do? I mean, I assumed Steve was going to remarry you, but . . ."

"Obviously that's out of the question."

"But . . ."

"Single women give birth every day. It's rather commonplace now for a woman to choose to raise a child on her own. That was my original intention."

"But, Steve . . ."

"Steve is out of my life." Her hand moved to her stomach and a soft smile courted the edges of her mouth. "He gave me what I wanted. Someday he'll be smart enough to calculate dates, but when he does it'll be too late."

"Oh, Carol, don't say that. Steve loves you so much."

"He's hurt me for the last time. He can't love me and accuse me of the things he has. It's over for us, and there's no going back."

"But he does love you." Lindy walked around a bit more and then plopped down across from Carol. "When he wouldn't talk to me on the phone, I went over to the apartment. I've never seen him like this. He frightened me."

"What's wrong?" Carol was angry with herself for caring, but she did.

"He'd been drinking heavily."

"That's not like Steve."

"I know," Lindy said heatedly. "I didn't know when he'd eaten last, so I fixed him something, which was a mistake because once he had something in his stomach he got feisty again and wanted me to leave."

"Did you?"

"No." Lindy started nibbling on the corner of her mouth. "I kept asking him questions about you, which only made him more angry. I soon learned you were a subject best avoided."

"I can imagine."

"After a while, he fell asleep on the sofa and I stayed around and cleaned up the apartment. It was a mess. Then . . . I heard Steve. I thought at first he was in the middle of a bad dream and I went to wake him, but when I came into the living room, I found him sitting on the end of the davenport with his hands over his face. He was weeping, Carol. As I've never seen a man weep before — heart-wrenching sobs that came from the deepest part of his soul. I can't even describe it to you."

Carol lowered her gaze to her hands, which had begun to tremble.

"This is the first time I've seen my brother cry, and his sobs tore straight through my heart. I couldn't stand by and do nothing. I wanted to comfort him and find out what had hurt him so badly. I'm his sister, for heaven's sake — he should be able to talk to me. But he didn't want me anywhere near him and ordered me out of the apartment. I left, but I haven't been able to stop thinking about it since."

A tear spilled out of the corner of Carol's eye and left a moist trail down the side of her face.

"By the time I got home I was crying, too. I don't know what to do anymore."

Carol's throat thickened. "There's nothing you can do. This is something Steve has to work out himself."

"Can't you talk to him?" Lindy pleaded. "He loves you so much and it's eating him alive."

"It won't do any good." Carol spoke from bitter experience.

"How can two people who obviously love each other let this happen?"

"I wish I knew." Carol's voice dropped to a whispered sob.

"What about Steve and the baby?"

"He doesn't want to have anything to do with this pregnancy. That's his decision, Lindy."

"But it's the wrong one! Surely you can get him to realize that."

She shook her head sadly. "Once Steve decides on something, his mind is set. He's too stubborn to listen to reason."

"But you love him."

"I wish I could deny that, but I do care about

him, with all my heart. Unfortunately that doesn't change a thing."

"How can you walk away from him like this?"

Carol's heart constricted with pain. "I've never left Steve. Not once. He's always been the one to walk away."

Chapter Eleven

"I'd do anything I could to make things right between me and Steve," Carol told Lindy, "but it isn't possible anymore."

"Why not?" Lindy pleaded. Carol knew it was hard for Lindy to understand when her own recent marriage was thriving. "You're both crazy in love with each other."

The truth in that statement was undeniable. Although Steve believed her capable of breaking her wedding vows and the worst kind of deceit, he continued to love her. For her part, Carol had little pride when it came to her ex-husband. She should have cut her losses the minute he'd accused her of having an affair, walked away from her and filed for the divorce. Instead she'd spent the next year of her life in limbo, licking her wounds, pretending the emotional scars had healed. It had taken Christmas Eve to show her how far she still had to go to get over loving Steve Kyle.

"You can't just walk away from him," Lindy pleaded. "What about the baby?"

"Steve doesn't want anything to do with my daughter."

"Give him time, Carol. You know Steve probably better than anyone. He can be such a stubborn fool sometimes. It just takes awhile for him to come to his senses. He'll wake up one morning and recognize the truth about the baby."

"I have to forget him for my own sanity." Carol stood, delivered her empty iced-tea glass to the kitchen and prepared to leave. There wasn't anything Lindy could say that would change the facts. Yes, she did love Steve and probably always would, but that didn't alter what he believed.

Lindy followed her to the front door. "If you need something, anything at all, please call me."

Carol nodded. "I will."

"Promise?"

"Promise." Carol knew that Lindy realized how difficult it was for her to ask for help. Impulsively she hugged Steve's sister. From now on, Lindy would be her only link to Steve and Carol was grateful for the friendship they shared.

Steve had to get out of the apartment before he went crazy. He'd spent the past few days drowning his misery in a bottle and the only thing it had brought him was more pain.

He showered, shaved and dressed. Walking would help clear his mind.

With no real destination in mind, he headed toward the waterfront. He got as far as Pike Place Market and aimlessly wandered among the thick crowds there. The colorful sights of the vegetable and meat displays and the sounds of cheerful vendors helped lift his spirits.

He bought a crisp, red Delicious apple and ate it as he ambled toward the booths that sold various craft items designed to attract the tourist trade. He paused and examined a sculpture made of volcanic ash from Mount Saint Helens. Another booth sold scenic photos of the Pacific Northwest, and another, thick, hand-knit Indian sweaters.

"Could I interest you in something?" a friendly older woman asked. Her long silver hair framed her face, and she offered him a wide smile.

"No thanks, I'm just looking." Steve paused and glanced over the items on her table. Sterling silver jewelry dotted a black velvet cloth — necklaces, earrings and rings of all sizes and shapes.

"You can't buy silver anywhere for my prices," the woman said.

"It's very nice."

"If jewelry doesn't interest you, perhaps these will." She stood and pulled a box of silver objects from beneath the table, lifting it up for him to inspect.

The first thing Steve noticed was a sterling-silver piggy bank. He smiled recalling how he and Carol had dumped their spare change in a piggy bank for months in an effort to save enough for a vacation to Hawaii. They'd spent it instead for the closing costs on the house.

"This is a popular item," the woman told him, bringing out a baby rattle. "Lots of jewelry stores sell these, but no one can beat my prices."

"How much?" Steve couldn't believe he'd asked. What the hell would he do with a baby rattle — especially one made of sterling silver.

The woman stated a reasonable price. "I'll take it," he said, astonished to hear the words come out of his mouth.

"Would you like one with blue ribbon or pink?"

Already Steve regretted the impulse. What was he planning to do? Give it to Carol? He'd decided the best thing for him to do as far as his ex-wife was concerned was to never see her again.

"Sir? Blue or pink?"

"Blue," he answered in a hoarse whisper. For the son he would probably never father. Blue for the color of Carol's eyes when she smiled at him.

By the time Steve walked back to the apartment, the sack containing the silver baby rattle felt like it weighed thirty pounds. By rights, he thought, he should toss the silly thing in the garbage. But he didn't.

He set it on the kitchen counter and opened the refrigerator, looking for something to eat, but nothing interested him. When he turned, the rattle seemed to draw his gaze. He stared at it for a long moment, yearning strongly to press it into the hand of his own child.

Blood thundered in his ears and his heart pounded so hard and fast that his chest ached. He would save the toy for Lindy and Rush whenever they had children, he decided.

Feeling only slightly better, he moved into the living room and turned on the television. He reached for the *TV Guide*, flipped through the pages, sighed and turned off the set. A second later, he rushed to his feet.

He didn't know who the hell he was trying to kid. That silver rattle with the pretty blue ribbon was for Carol and her baby, and it was going to torment him until he got rid of it.

He could mail her the toy and be done with the plaything. Or have Lindy give it to her without letting Carol know it had come from him. Or . . . or he could just set it on the porch and let her find it.

The last idea appealed to him. He would casually drive by her neighborhood, park his car around the block and wait until it was dark enough to sneak up and leave the rattle on the front step. He was the last person she would ever suspect would do something like that.

With his plan formulated, Steve drove to Carol's house. He was half a block away from her place when he noticed her car. She was leaving. This would work out even better. He could follow her and when she got where she was going, he could place the rattle inside her car. That way she would assume someone had mistaken her car for their own and inadvertently set the rattle inside. There wasn't anything she could do but take it home with her.

Carol headed north on Interstate 5, and her destination was a matter of simple deduction. She was going to the Northgate Mall. Lord, that woman loved to shop. The minute she steered onto the freeway on-ramp, Steve knew exactly where she was headed. They'd been married for five years, and their year apart hadn't changed her. The smug knowledge produced a smile.

But Carol exited before the mall.

Steve's heart started to pound. He was three cars behind her, but if she wasn't going shopping, he didn't know what she was planning. Maybe she was rendezvousing with Todd. Maybe all those times she'd told him she was shopping Carol had actually been meeting with her employer. The muscles in his stomach clenched into a knot so tight and painful that it stole his breath.

If there'd been any way to turn the car around, Steve would have done it, but he was trapped in the center lane of traffic and forced to follow the heavy flow.

It wasn't until they'd gone several blocks that Steve noticed the back side of the mall. Perhaps she'd found a shortcut and had never bothered to tell him about it.

Carol turned onto a busy side street, and against his better judgment, he followed her. A few minutes later, when Carol turned into the large parking lot at Northgate Mall, Steve felt almost giddy with relief.

She parked close to the JCPenney store, and Steve eased his vehicle into a slot four spaces over. On a whim, he decided to follow her inside. He'd always wondered what women found so intriguing about shopping.

He was far enough behind her on the escalator to almost lose her. Standing at the top, he searched until he found her standing in women's fashions, sorting through a rack of dresses. It took him a minute to realize they were maternity dresses. Although she'd lost several pounds, she must be having difficulty finding things that fit her, he realized. According to his calculations, she was five months pregnant — probably closer to six.

He lounged around while she took a handful of bright spring dresses and moved into the changing room. Fifteen minutes passed before she returned, and to Steve it felt like a lifetime.

When she returned, she went back to the rack and replaced all but one of the dresses. She held up a pretty blue one with a wide sailor's collar and red tie and studied it carefully. Apparently she changed her mind because she hung it back up with the others. Still she lingered an extra minute, continuing to examine the outfit. She ran her fingers down the sleeve to catch the price tag, read it, shook her head and reluctantly walked away.

The minute she was out of sight, Steve was at the clothing rack. Obviously she wanted the dress, yet she hadn't bought it. He checked the price tag and frowned. It was moderately priced, certainly not exorbitant. If she wanted it, which she apparently did, then she should have it.

For the second time in the same day, Steve found himself making a purchase that was difficult to rationalize. It wasn't as if he had any use for a maternity dress. But why not? he asked himself. If he left the rattle in her car it shouldn't make any difference if he added a dress. It wasn't likely that she would tie him to either purchase. Let her think her fairy godmother was gifting her.

From his position at the cash register, Steve saw Carol walk through the infant's department. She ran her hand over the top rail of a white Jenny Lind crib and examined it with a look of such sweet anticipation that Steve felt guilty for invading her privacy.

"Would you like this dress on the hanger or in a sack?" the salesclerk asked him.

It took Steve a moment to realize she was talking to him. "A sack, please." He couldn't very well walk through the mall carrying a maternity dress.

Carol bought something, too, but Steve couldn't see what it was. Infant T-shirts or something like that, he guessed. His vantage point in the furniture department wasn't the best. Carol started to walk toward him, and he turned abruptly and pretended to be testing out a recliner.

Apparently she didn't see him, and he settled into the seat and expelled a sigh of relief.

"Can I help you?" a salesclerk asked.

"Ah, no, thanks," he said, getting to his feet.

Carol headed down the escalator, and Steve scooted around a couple of women pushing baby strollers in an effort not to lose sight of her.

Carol's steps were filled with purpose as she moved down the wide aisle to women's shoes. She picked up a red low-heeled dress shoe that was on display, but when the clerk approached, she smiled and shook her head. Within a couple of minutes she was on her way.

Feeling more like a fool with every minute, Steve followed her out of the store and into the heart of the mall. The place was packed, as it generally was on Saturday afternoon. Usually Steve avoided the mall on weekends, preferring to do his shopping during the day or at night.

He saw Carol stop at a flower stand and buy herself a red rosebud. She'd always been fond of flowers, and he was pleased that she treated herself to something special.

She'd gone only a few steps when he noticed that her steps had slowed.

Something was wrong. He could tell from the way she walked. He cut across to the other side, where the flow of shoppers was heading in the opposite direction. Feeling like a secret government agent, he pressed himself against the storefront in an effort to watch her more closely. She had pressed her hand to her abdomen and her face had gone deathly pale. She was in serious pain, he determined as a sense of alarm filled him. Steve could feel it as strongly as if he were the one suffering.

Although he was certain she had full view of him, Carol didn't notice. She cut across the streams of shoppers to the benches that lined the middle of the concourse and sat. Her shoulders moved up and down as though she were taking in deep breaths in an effort to control her reaction to whatever was happening. She closed her eyes and bit her lower lip.

The alarm turned to panic. He didn't know what to do. He couldn't rush up to her and demand to know what was wrong. Nor could he casually stroll by and pretend he just happened to be shopping and had stumbled upon her. But something needed to be done — someone had to help her.

Steve had never felt more helpless in his life. Not knowing what else he could do, he walked up and plopped himself down next to her.

"Hi," he said in a falsely cheerful voice.

"Steve." She looked at him, her eyes brimming with tears. She reached for his hand, gripping it so hard her nails cut into his flesh.

All pretense was gone, wiped away by the stampeding fear he sensed in her.

"What's wrong?"

She shook her head. "I . . . I don't know."

Her eyes widened and he was struck by how yellow her skin was. He took her hand in both of his. "You're in pain?"

She nodded. Her fear palatable. "I'm so afraid."

"What do you want me to do?" He debated on whether he should could call for an ambulance or contact her doctor and have him meet them at the hospital.

"I . . . don't know what's wrong. I've had this pain twice, but it's always gone away after a couple of minutes." She closed her eyes. "Oh, Steve, I'm so afraid I'm going to lose my baby."

Chapter Twelve

Restless, Steve paced the corridor of the maternity ward in Overlake Hospital, his hands stuffed inside his pants pockets. He felt as though he were carrying the world on his shoulders. Each passing minute tightened the knot in his stomach until he was consumed with worry and dread.

He wanted to see Carol — he longed to talk to her — but there wasn't anything more for him to say. He'd done what he could for her, and by rights he should leave. But he couldn't walk away from her. Not now. Not when she needed him.

Not knowing what else to do, he found a pay phone and contacted his sister.

"Lindy, it's Steve."

"Steve, how are you? I'm so glad you phoned; I haven't stopped thinking about you."

She sounded so pleased to hear from him, and he swallowed down his guilt for the way he'd treated her. He'd been rude and unreasonable when she'd only been showing concern for him.

"I'm fine," he said hurriedly, "Listen, I'm at Overlake Hospital . . ."

"You're at the hospital? You're fine, but you're at Overlake? Good God, what happened? I knew it, I just knew something like this was going to happen. I felt it . . ."

"Lindy, shut up for a minute, would you?"

"No, I won't shut up — I'm family, Steve Kyle. Family. If you can't come to me when you're hurting, just who can you go to? You seem to think I'm too young to know anything about emotional pain, but you're wrong. When Paul dumped me it wasn't any Sunday-school picnic."

"I'm not the one in need of medical attention — it's Carol."

"Carol!" His blurted announcement seemed to sweep away all his sister's pent-up frustration. "What's wrong?" she asked quietly.

"I don't exactly know; the doctor's still with her. I think she might be losing the baby. She needs a woman — I'm the last person who should be here. I didn't know who else to call. Can you come?"

"Of course. I'll be there as fast as I can."

It seemed as though no more than a couple of minutes had passed before Lindy came rushing down the hall. He stood at the sight of her, immensely grateful. Relief washed over him and he wrapped his arms around her.

"The doctor hasn't come out yet," he explained before she could ask. He released her and checked his watch. "It's been over an hour now."

"What happened?"

"I'm not sure. Carol started having some

kind of abdominal pains. I phoned her gynecologist, and after I explained what was happening, he suggested we meet him here."

"You said you thought Carol might be having a miscarriage?"

"Good Lord, I don't know anything about this woman stuff. All I can tell you is that she was in agony. I did the only thing I could — I got her here." The ten minutes it took to get Carol to the emergency room had been emotionally draining. She was terrified of losing the baby and had wept almost uncontrollably. Through her sobs she'd told him how much she wanted her baby and how this pregnancy would be her only opportunity. Little of what she'd said had made sense to Steve. He'd tried to find the words to assure her, but he hadn't really known what to say.

Just then Steve noticed Carol's physician, Dr. Stewart, push open the swinging door and walk toward the waiting area. He met him halfway.

"How is she?" he asked, his heart in his throat.

The gynecologist rubbed his hand down the side of his jaw and shook his head. His frown crowded his brows together. "She's as good as can be expected."

"The baby?"

"The pregnancy is progressing nicely . . . thus far."

Although the child wasn't his and Carol had tried to trick him into believing otherwise,

Steve still felt greatly relieved knowing that her baby wasn't in any immediate danger.

"I'm sorry to keep you waiting so long, but quite frankly Carol's symptoms had me stumped. It's unusual for someone her age to suffer from this sort of problem."

"What problem?" Lindy blurted out.

"Gall bladder."

"Gall bladder," Steve repeated frowning. He didn't know what he'd expected, but it certainly hadn't been that.

"She tells me she's been suffering from flulike symptoms, which she accepted as morning sickness. There wasn't any reason for either of us to assume otherwise. Some of her other discomforts can be easily misinterpreted as well.

"The most serious threat at the moment is that she's dangerously close to being dehydrated. Predictably that has prompted other health risks."

"What do you mean?" Lindy asked.

"Her sodium and potassium levels have dropped and her heart rate is erratic. I've started an IV and that problem should take care of itself within a matter of hours."

"What's going to happen?"

Once more, Dr. Stewart ran a hand down the side of his face and shook his head. His kind eyes revealed his concern. "I've called in a surgeon friend of mine, and we're going to do a few more preliminary tests. But from what I'm seeing at this point, I don't think we can put off operating. Her gall bladder appears to be acutely swollen and is causing an obstruction."

"If you do the surgery, what will happen to the baby?" For Carol's sake, Steve prayed for the tiny life she was carrying.

Dr. Stewart's sober expression turned grim. "There's always a risk to the pregnancy when anesthesia is involved. I'd like to delay this, but I doubt that we can. Under normal conditions gall-bladder surgery can be scheduled at a patient's convenience, but not in Carol's case, I fear. But I want you to know, we'll do everything I can to save the child."

"Please try." Carol had looked at him with such terror and helplessness that he couldn't help being affected. He would do everything humanly possible to see that she carried this child to full term.

"Please do what you can," Lindy added her own plea. "This child means a great deal to her."

Dr. Stewart nodded. "Carol's sleeping now, but you can see her for a couple of minutes, if you'd like. One at a time."

Steve looked to Lindy, who gestured for him to go in first. He smiled his appreciation and followed the grandfatherly doctor into Carol's room.

As Dr. Stewart had explained, she was sleeping soundly. She looked incredibly fragile with tubes stretching down from an IV pole to connect with the veins in her arm.

Steve stood beside her for several minutes, loving her completely. Emotion clogged his throat and he turned away. He loved her; he always would. No matter what had happened in the past, he couldn't imagine a future without Carol.

"How is she?" Lindy asked when he came out of the room.

He found he couldn't answer her with anything more than a short nod.

Lindy disappeared and returned five minutes later. By then Steve had had a chance to form a plan of action, and he felt better for it.

As Lindy stepped toward him, he held her gaze with newfound determination. He and Carol were both fools if they thought they could stay apart. It wasn't going to work. Without Carol he was only half-alive. And she'd admitted how miserable she'd been during their year's separation.

"I'm going to marry her," Steve informed his sister brusquely.

"What?" Lindy looked at him as though she'd misheard him.

"I'm going to get the chaplain to come to the hospital, and I'm going to marry Carol."

Lindy studied him for several moments. "Don't you think she should have some say in this?"

"Yes . . . no."

"But I thought . . . Carol told me you didn't

believe the baby is yours."

"It isn't."

Lindy rolled her eyes, then shook her head, her features tight with impatience. "That is the most ridiculous thing you've ever said. Honestly, Steve, where do you come up with these crazy ideas?"

"What idea? That the baby isn't mine, or re-marrying Carol?"

"Both!"

"Whether or not I'm the father doesn't make one bit of difference. I've decided it doesn't matter. From here on out, I'm claiming her child as mine."

"But . . ."

"I don't care. I love Carol and I'll learn to love her baby. That's the end of it." Once the decision had been made, it felt right. The two of them had played a fool's game for over a year, but no more — he wouldn't stand for it. "I'm not going to put up with any arguments from you or from Carol. I want her as my wife — we were wrong ever to have gone through with the divorce. All I'm doing now is correcting a mistake that should never have happened," he told his sister in a voice that men jumped to obey.

Lindy took a moment to digest his words. "Don't you think you should discuss this in a rational matter with Carol? Don't you think she should have some input into her own life?"

"I suppose. But she needs me — although

she isn't likely to admit it."

"You've had just as difficult a time recognizing that fact yourself."

"Not anymore."

"When do you plan to tell her?"

Steve didn't know. He'd only reached this conclusion in the last five minutes, but already he felt in control of his life again.

"Well?" his sister pressed.

"I haven't figured out when. . . . Before the surgery, I think, if it can be arranged."

"Steve, you're not thinking clearly. Carol isn't going to want to be married sitting in a hospital bed, looking all sickly and pale."

"The sooner we get this settled the better."

"For whom?" Lindy prompted.

"For both of us."

Lindy threw up her hands. "Sometimes the things you say utterly shock me."

"They do?" Steve didn't care — he felt as if he could float out of the hospital, he was so relieved. Carol would probably come through the surgery with flying colors and everything would fall into place the way it should have long ago. This had certainly been a crazy day. He'd bought a sterling silver rattle, followed Carol around a shopping mall like an FBI agent, driven her to the hospital, then made a decision that would go a long way toward assuring their happy future. Steve sighed deeply, feeling suddenly weary.

"Is there any other bombshell you'd care to

hit me with?" Lindy asked teasingly.

Steve paused and then surprised her by nodding. Some of the happiness he'd experienced earlier vanished. There was one other decision he'd made — one not as pleasant but equally necessary.

"Should I sit down for this one?" Lindy asked, still grinning. She slipped her arm around his waist and looked up at him.

"I don't think so."

"Well, don't keep me in suspense, big brother."

Steve regarded her soberly. "I'm leaving the Navy."

Chapter Thirteen

Carol opened her eyes slowly. The room was dim, the blinds over the window closed. She frowned when her gaze fell on the IV stand, and she tried to raise herself.

"You're in the hospital." Steve's voice was warm and caressing.

She lowered her head back to the pillow and turned toward the sound. Steve stood at her bedside. From the ragged, tired look about him, she guessed he'd been standing there all night.

"How long have you been here?" she asked hoarsely, testing her tongue.

"Not very long."

She closed her eyes and grinned. "You never could tell a decent lie."

He brushed the hair from her cheek and his fingers lingered on her face as though he needed to touch her. She knew she should ask him to leave, but his presence comforted her. She needed him. She didn't know how he'd happened to be at Northgate Mall, but she would always be grateful he'd found her when he did.

Her hand moved to her stomach, and she flattened it there. "The baby's all right?"

Steve didn't answer her for a moment, and a

sickening sense of dread filled her. Her eyes flew open. The doctor had repeatedly assured her that the baby was safe, but something might have happened while she had slept. She'd been out for hours and much of what had taken place after they arrived at the hospital remained foggy in her mind.

"Everything's fine with the pregnancy."

"Thank God," she whispered fervently.

"Dr. Stewart said you were near exhaustion." He reached for her hand and laced his fingers with hers. His thumb worked back and forth on the inside of her wrist.

"I think I could sleep for a week," Carol said, her voice starting to sound more sure. It seemed as though it had been years since she'd had a decent rest. Even before her pregnancy had been confirmed she'd felt physically and emotionally drained, as if she were running on a treadmill, working as fast as her legs would carry her and getting nowhere.

"How do you feel now?"

Carol had to think about it. "Different. I don't know how to describe it. I'm not exactly sick and I'm not in any pain, but something's not right, either."

"You should have recognized that weeks ago. According to Dr. Stewart, you've probably been feeling ill for months."

"They know what's causing the problem?" Her heart started to work doubly hard. Not until the severe attack of pain in the shopping mall had she been willing to admit something could be wrong with her.

"Dr. Stewart thinks it could be your gall bladder."

"My what?"

"Gall bladder," he repeated softly. "I'm sure he can explain it far better than I can, but from what I understand it's a pear-shaped pouch close to the liver."

Carol arched her brows at his attempt at humor and offered him a weak smile. "That explains it."

Steve grinned back at her, and for a moment everything went still. His eyes held such tenderness that she dared to hope again — dared to believe he'd discovered the truth about her and their baby. Dared to let the love that was stored in her heart shine through her eyes.

"I never thought I'd see you again," she said, and her voice quivered with emotion.

Steve lowered his gaze briefly. "I couldn't stay away. I love you too much."

"Oh, Steve, how could we do this to each other? You think such terrible things of me and I can't bear it anymore. I keep telling myself the baby and I would be better off without you, and then I feel only half alive. When we're separated, nothing feels right in my life — nothing is good."

"When I'm not with you, I'm only a shell." He raised her hand to his lips and kissed her knuckles.

Carol felt the tears gather in her eyes and she turned her head away, unwilling to have Steve witness her emotion. No man would ever be more right for her, and no man could ever be so wrong.

She heard the sound of a chair being pushed to the side of the bed. "I want us to remarry," he said firmly. "I've thought it over. In fact, I haven't thought of anything else in the past fifteen hours — and I'm convinced this is the right thing for us to do."

Carol knew it was right, too. "But what about the baby?" she whispered. "You think —"

"From this moment on, the child is mine in my heart and in my soul. He's a part of you and that's the only important thing."

"She," Carol corrected absently. "I'm having a girl."

"Okay . . . whatever you want as long as we're together."

Carol's mind flooded with arguments, but she hadn't the strength to fight him. The intervening months would convince Steve that this child was his far better than any eloquent speeches she could give him now. By the time the baby was born, his doubts would have vanished completely. In the meantime they would find a way to settle matters — that was essential because they were both so miserable apart.

"Will you marry me, Carol, a second time?"

"I want to say yes. Everything within me is telling me it's the right thing to do . . . for me and for the baby. But I'm frightened, too."

"I'm going to be a good husband and father, I promise you that."

"I know you will."

"I made another decision yesterday — one that will greatly affect both our lives." His hand pressed against the side of her face and gently brushed the hair from her temple. "I'm leaving the Navy."

Carol couldn't believe her ears. The military was Steve's life; it had been his goal from the time he was a teenager. His dream. He'd never wanted to be or do anything else.

"But you love your work."

"I love you more," he countered.

"It's not an either-or situation, Steve. I've lived all these years as a Navy wife, I've adjusted."

A hint of a smile touched his face. "I won't be separated from you again."

For Steve's sake, Carol had always put on a happy face and seen him off with a cheerful wave, but she'd hated the life, dreading their months apart. Always had and always would. The promise of a more conventional marriage seemed too good to be true. Her head was swimming at the thought of him working a nine-to-five job. She wanted this — she wanted it badly.

"You're the most important person in my life. I'm getting out of the Navy so I can be the kind of husband and father I should be."

"Oh, Steve." The joy that cascaded through her at that moment brought tears to her eyes.

"I can't think of any other way to show you how serious I am."

Neither could Carol. Nevertheless his announcement worried her. Navy life was in Steve's blood, and she didn't know if he could find happiness outside the only career he'd ever known.

"Let's not make such a major decision now," she suggested reluctantly. "There'll be plenty of time to talk about this later."

Steve's eyes filled with tenderness. "Whatever you say."

Humming softly, a nurse wandered into the room and greeted them. "Good morning."

"Morning," Carol answered.

The room was bathed in the soft light of day as the middle-aged woman opened the blinds.

"I'm sorry, but there won't be any breakfast for you this morning. Dr. Stewart will be in later, and I'm sure he'll schedule something for you to eat this afternoon."

Carol didn't feel the least bit hungry. Her appetite had been almost nonexistent for months.

"I'll check on you in an hour," the woman said on her way out the door.

Carol nodded. "Thank you." She was filled with nagging questions about what was going to happen. Naturally she hoped Dr. Stewart could give her a prescription and send her home, but she had the feeling she was being overly optimistic.

Steve must have read the doubt in her eyes because he said, "From what Dr. Stewart told me, he's going to have you complete a series of tests this morning. Following those, we'll be able to make a decision."

"What kind of tests? What kind of decision?"

"Honey, I don't know, but don't worry. I'm not leaving you — not for a minute."

Carol hated to be such a weakling, but she was frightened. "Whatever happens, whatever they have to do, I can take it," she said a little shakily.

"I know you can, love. I know you can."

As promised, for the next few hours Carol underwent several tests. She was pinched, poked and prodded and wheeled to several corners of the hospital. As Steve promised, he was with her each time they took her into another and waiting when she returned.

"Quit looking so worried," she told him, when she'd been wheeled back to her room once more. "I'm going to be fine."

"I know."

She slept after that and woke late in the afternoon. Once more Steve was at her bedside, leaning forward, his face in his hands.

"Bad news?" she asked.

He smiled and Carol could tell by the stiff way his mouth moved that the action was forced.

"What's wrong?" she demanded.

He stood and came to stand beside her. She gave him her hand, her eyes wide with fear.

"Dr. Stewart assured me that under normal conditions, gall bladder surgery is optional. But not in your case. Your gall bladder is acutely swollen and is causing several complications to vital organs. It has to be removed, and the sooner the better."

Carol expelled her breath and nodded. She'd feared something like this, but she was young and healthy and strong; everything would be fine.

"He's called in a surgeon and they've scheduled the operating room for you first thing tomorrow morning."

Carol swallowed her worry. "I can handle that."

"This isn't minor surgery, Carol. I don't think you'd appreciate me minimizing the risks."

"No . . . no, I wouldn't."

"Dr. Stewart and his associate will be back later today to explain the details of what they'll be doing. It's major surgery, but you have several things in your favor."

She nodded, appreciating the fact that she would know precisely what the medical team would be doing to her body.

"What about the baby?"

Steve's expression tightened and he lifted his eyes from hers. "The pregnancy poses a problem."

"What kind of problem?"

"If the surgery could be delayed, Dr. Stewart would prefer to do that, but it can't be. Your life is at risk."

"What about the pregnancy?" Carol demanded. "I'm not agreeing to anything until I hear what will happen to my baby."

Steve's eyes revealed myriad emotions. Worry and fear dominated, but there was something else — something that took her an extended moment to analyze. Something that clouded his features and ravaged his face. Regret, she decided, then quickly changed her mind. It was more than that — a deep inner sorrow, even remorse.

When Steve spoke, it was as if each word had to be tugged from his mouth. "I'm not going to coat the truth. There's a chance the anesthesia will terminate the pregnancy."

"I won't do it," she cried automatically. "The whole thing's off. I'm not doing anything that will hurt my baby."

"Carol, listen to reason . . ."

"No." She twisted her head so that she wouldn't have to look at him. As long as she drew a single breath there was no way she would agree to do anything that would harm her daughter.

"Honey," he whispered. "We don't have any choice. If we delay the surgery, you could die."

"Then so be it."

"No." He almost shouted the word. "There's

a risk to the baby, but one we're both going to have to take. There's no other choice."

She closed her eyes, unwilling to argue with him further. Her mind was made up.

"Carol, I don't like this any better than you do."

She refused to look at him and pinched her lips together, determined not to murmur a single word. Nothing he could say would change her mind.

The silence in the room was magnified to deafening proportions.

"I love you, Carol, and I can't allow you to chance your life for a baby. If the worst happens and the pregnancy is terminated, then we'll have to accept it. There'll be other children — lots more — and the next time there won't be any question about who the father is."

If Steve had driven a stake into her heart, he couldn't have hurt her more. No words had ever been more cruel. No wonder he was so willing to tell her he'd decided to accept this child as his own. She would likely lose the baby, and believing what he did, Steve no doubt felt that was for the best.

Carol jerked her head around so fast she nearly dislocated her neck. "The next time there won't be any questions?" she repeated in a small, still voice.

"I know this is painful for you, but —"

"I want *this* baby."

"Carol, please . . ."

"How long have you known about this danger?"

Steve looked stunned by her anger. "Dr. Stewart told me about the possibility after I brought you to the hospital yesterday."

Exactly what she'd expected. Everything Steve had done, everything he'd said from that point on was suddenly suspect. He wanted them to remarry and he was going to leave the Navy. His reasoning became as clear as water to her: he didn't really long for a change in their life-style, nor had his offer to leave the Navy been a decision based on his desire to build a strong marital relationship. He didn't dread their separations as she always had — he'd thrived on them. But if he wasn't in the military, then he could spend his days watching her. There would be no opportunity for her to have an affair. And when she became pregnant a second time, he would have the assurance that the baby was indeed his. His offer hadn't been made from love but from fear rooted in a lack of trust.

It amazed her, now that she thought about it, that he would be willing to give up such a promising career for her. He really did love her, in his own way, but not enough. Ultimately he would regret his decision, and so would she. But by then it would be too late.

"I'm probably doing a bad job of this," he said, and rammed his fingers through his hair. "I should have let Dr. Stewart explain everything to you."

"No," she said dispassionately. "What you've told me explains a good deal. You've been completely up-front with me and I appreciate what it cost you to tell me this. I . . . I think it's my turn to be honest with you now."

A dark frown contorted his features. "Carol . . ."

"No, it's time you finally learned the truth. I hesitated when you asked me to marry you and there's a reason. You don't need to worry about me, Steve. You never had to. My baby's father has promised to take care of me. When my plan to trick you didn't work, I contacted him and told him I was pregnant. He thought about it for a couple of days and has decided to marry me himself. I appreciate your offer, but it isn't necessary."

Steve looked as if she'd slipped a knife into his stomach.

"You're lying."

"No, for once I'm telling you the truth. Go back to your life and I'll go on with mine. We'll both be far happier this way."

He didn't move for several minutes. His hands curved around the raised railing at the side of the bed and she swore his grip was strong enough to permanently mark the bars. His eyes hardened to chips of glacial ice.

"Who is the father?" he demanded.

Carol closed her eyes, determined not to answer.

"Who is he?"

She looked away, but his fingers closed

around her chin and forced her face back toward him.

"Todd?"

She was sick of hearing that name. "No."

"Who?"

"No one you know," she shouted.

"Is he married?"

"No."

A pounding, vibrating silence followed.

"Is this what you really want?"

"Yes," she told him. "Yes. . . ."

A year seemed to pass before she heard him leave the room. When he did, each step he took away from her sounded like nails being pounded into a coffin.

It was finished. There was no going back now. Steve Kyle was out of her life and she'd made certain he would never come back.

Carol felt as if she were walking through a thick bog, every step was hindered, her progress painstakingly slow. A mist rose from the marsh, blocking her view, and she struggled to look into the distance, seeking the light, but she was met instead by more fog.

A soft cry — like that of a small animal — reverberated around her, and it took her a minute to realize she was the one who had made the sound.

She wasn't in any pain. Not physically anyway.

The agony she suffered came from deep inside — a weight of grief so heavy no human should ever be expected to carry it. Carol couldn't understand what had happened or why she felt this crippling sense of loss.

Then it came to her.

Her baby . . . they couldn't delay the surgery. The fog parted and a piece of her memory slipped into place. Steve had walked away from her, and soon after he'd gone she'd suffered another attack that had doubled her over with excruciating pain. The hospital staff had called for Dr. Stewart and surgery had been arranged immediately. The option of waiting for even one day had been taken out of her hands.

Now Steve was out of her life and she'd lost her baby, too.

Moisture ran down the side of her face, but when she tried to lift her hand, she found she hadn't the strength.

A sob came, wrenched from her soul. There would be no more children for her. She was destined to live alone for the rest of her life.

"Nurse, do something. She's in pain."

The words drifted from a great distance, and she tossed her head to and fro in an effort to discover the source. She saw no one in the fog. No one.

Once more the debilitating sense of loneliness overtook her and she was alone. Whoever had been there had left her to find her own way through the darkness.

More sobs came — her own, she realized —

erupting in deafening sound all around her.

Then she felt something — a hand she thought — warm and gentle, press over her abdomen. The weight of it was a comfort she couldn't describe.

"Your baby's alive," the voice told her. "Can you feel him? He's going to live and so are you!"

It was a voice of authority, a voice of a man who spoke with confidence; a voice few would question.

A familiar voice.

The dark fog started to close in again and Carol wanted to shout for it to stop. She stumbled toward the light, but it was shut off from her, and she found herself trapped in a black void, defenseless and lost. She didn't know if she would ever have the strength to escape it.

A persistent squeak interrupted Carol's sleep. A wheel far off in the distance was badly in need of oil. The irritating ruckus grew louder until Carol decided it would be useless to try to ignore it any longer.

She opened her eyes to discover Steve's sister standing over her.

"Lindy?"

"Carol, oh, Carol, you're awake."

"Shouldn't I be?" she asked. Her former sister-in-law looked as if she were about to burst into tears.

"I can't believe it. We've been so worried. . . .

No one thought you were going to make it." Lindy cupped her hands over her mouth and nose. "We nearly lost you, Carol Kyle!"

"You did?" This was news to her. She had little memory. The dreadful pain had returned — she remembered that. And then she'd been trapped in that marsh, lost and confused, but it hadn't felt so bad. She had been hot — so terribly hot — she recalled, but there were pleasant memories there, too. Someone had called out to her from there, assured her. She couldn't place what the voice had said, but she remembered how she'd struggled to walk toward the sound of it. The voice hadn't always been comforting. Carol recalled how one time it had shouted at her, harsh and demanding. She hadn't wanted to obey it then and had tried to escape, but the voice had followed her relentlessly, refusing to leave her alone.

"How do you feel?"

"Like I've been asleep for a week."

"Make that two."

"Two?" Carol echoed, shocked. "That long?"

"All right, *almost* two weeks. It's actually been ten days. You had emergency surgery and then everything that could go wrong did. Oh, Carol, you nearly died."

"My baby's okay, isn't she?" From somewhere deep inside her heart came the reassurance that whatever else had happened, the child had survived. Carol vividly remembered the voice telling her so.

"Your baby is one hell of a little fighter."

Carol smiled. "Good."

Lindy moved a chair closer to the bed and sat down. "The doctor said he felt you'd come out of it today. You made a turn for the better around midnight."

"What time is it now?"

Lindy checked her watch. "About 9:00 a.m."

Already her eyes felt incredibly heavy. "I think I could sleep some more."

"As well you should."

Carol tried to smile. "So my daughter is a fighter. . . . Maybe I'll name her Sugar Ray Kyle."

"Go ahead and get some rest. I'll be here when you wake up."

Already Carol felt herself drifting off, but it was a pleasant sensation. The warm black folds closed their arms around her in a welcoming embrace.

When she stirred a second time, she discovered Lindy was at her bedside reading.

"Is this a vigil or something?" she asked, grinning. "Every time I wake up, you're here."

"I wanted to be sure you were really coming out of it," Lindy told her.

"I feel much better."

"You *look* much better."

The inside of her mouth felt like a sewer. "Do you have any idea how long it'll be before I can go home?"

"You won't. You're coming to live with Rush

and me for a couple of weeks until you regain your strength. And we won't take no for an answer."

"But —"

"No arguing!" Lindy's smile softened her brook-no-nonsense tone.

"I don't deserve a friend as good as you," Carol murmured, awed by Lindy's generosity.

"We should be sisters, and you know it."

Carol chose not to answer that. She preferred to push any thoughts of her ex-husband from her mind.

"This probably isn't the time to talk about Steve."

It wasn't, but Carol didn't stop her.

"I don't know what you said to him, but he doesn't seem to think you want to see him again. Carol, he's been worried sick over you. Won't you at least talk to him?"

A lump the size of a goose egg formed in her throat. "No," she whispered. "I don't want to have anything to do with Steve. We're better off divorced."

Chapter Fourteen

"I'm not an invalid," Carol insisted, frowning at her ex-sister-in-law as she carried her own breakfast dishes to the sink.

"But you've only been out of the hospital a week," Lindy argued, flittering around her like a mother hen protecting her smallest chick.

"For heaven's sake, sit down," Carol cried, "before you drive me crazy!"

"All right, all right."

Carol shared a knowing smile with Rush Callaghan, Lindy's husband. He was a different man than the Rush Carol had known before his marriage to Lindy. He smiled openly now. Laughed. Carol had been fond of Rush, but he'd always been so very serious — all Navy. The military wouldn't find a man more loyal than Rush, but loving Lindy had changed him — and for the better. Lindy had brought sunshine and laughter into his life and brightened his world in a wide spectrum of rainbow colors.

"Come on, Lindy," Rush said, "you can walk me to the door and kiss me goodbye."

With an eagerness that made Carol smile, her good friend escorted Rush to the front door and lingered there several minutes.

When she returned, Lindy walked blindly into the kitchen, wearing a dazed, contented grin. She plopped herself down in a chair, reached for her empty coffee cup and sighed. "He'll be gone for a couple of days."

"Are you going to suffer those Navy blues?"

"I suppose," Lindy said. She lifted her mug and rested her elbows on the table. "I'm a little giddy this morning because Rush and I reached a major decision last night." She smiled and the sun seemed to shine through her eyes. "We're going to start a family. Our first wedding anniversary is coming up soon, and we thought this would be a good way to celebrate."

"Sweet potatoes," Carol said, grinning from ear to ear. "They worked for me."

Lindy gave her a look that insinuated that perhaps Carol should return to the hospital for much-needed psychiatric treatment. "What was that?"

"Sweet potatoes. You know — yams. I heard a medical report over the news last year that reported the results of a study done on a tribe in Africa whose diet staple was sweet potatoes. The results revealed a higher estrogen level in the women and they attributed that fact to the yams."

"I see."

Lindy continued to study her closely. Carol giggled. "I'm not joking! They really work. I wanted to get pregnant and I couldn't count on anything more from Steve than Christmas Eve, so I ate enough sweet potatoes for my body to float in the hormone."

"One night did it?" Lindy's interest was piqued, although she struggled not to show it.

"Two actually — but who knows how long it would have taken otherwise. I ate that vegetable in every imaginable form — including some I wouldn't recommend. If you want, I'll loan you my collection of recipes."

A slow smile spread over Lindy's face, catching in her lovely brown eyes. "I want!"

Carol rinsed her plate and stuck it inside the dishwasher.

"Let me do that!" Lindy insisted, jumping to her feet. "Honest to goodness, Carol. You're so stubborn."

"No, please, I want to help. It makes me feel like I'm being useful." She never had been one to sit and do nothing. This period of convalescence had been troubling enough without Lindy babying her.

"You're recovering from major surgery for heaven's sake!" Steve's sister insisted.

"I'm fine."

"Now, maybe, but a week ago. . . ."

Even now Carol had a difficult time realizing how close she'd come to losing her life. It was the voice that had pulled her back, refusing to let her slip into the darkness, the voice that had urged her to live. Something deep within her subconscious had demanded she cling to life when it would have been so easy to surrender.

"Lindy, I need to ask you something." Unexpectedly Carol's mind was buzzing with doubts about the future.

"Sure, what is it?"

"If anything were to happen to me after the baby's born —"

"Nothing's going to happen to you," Lindy argued.

"Probably not." Carol pulled out the kitchen chair and sat down. She didn't want to sound as though she had a death wish, but with the baby came a responsibility she hadn't thought of before her illness. "I don't have much in the way of family. My mother died several years ago — soon after Steve . . . soon after I was married. She and my father were divorced years before, and I hardly know him. He has another family and I rarely hear from him."

Lindy nodded. "Dr. Elgin, the surgeon, asked us to contact any close family members and Steve phoned your father. He . . . he couldn't come."

"He's a busy man," Carol said, willingly offering an excuse for her father, the way she had for most of her life. "But if I were to die," she persisted, "there'd be no one to raise my baby."

"Steve . . ."

Carol shook her head. "No. He'll probably marry again and have his own family someday. And if he doesn't, he'll be so involved in the Navy he won't be much good for raising a child." It was so much to ask of anyone, even a friend as near and dear as Lindy. "Would you and Rush consider being her guardians?"

"Of course, Carol," Lindy assured her warmly. "But nothing's going to happen to you."

Carol smiled. "I certainly plan on living a long, productive life, but something like this surgery hits close to home."

"I'll talk it over with Rush, but I'm sure he'll be more than willing for us to be your baby's guardians."

"Thank you," Carol said, and impulsively hugged Lindy. Steve's family had always been good to her.

"Okay, now that that's settled, how about a hot game of gin rummy? I feel lucky."

"Sure . . ." Carol paused and her eyes rounded. Her hand moved to the slight curve of her stomach as her heart filled with happiness.

"Are you all right?"

"I'm fine. The baby just moved — she does that quite a bit now — but never this strong."

"Does it hurt?"

Carol shook her head. "Not in the least. I don't know how to describe it, but every time she decides to explore her little world, I get excited. In four short months I'll be holding my daughter. Oh, Lindy, I can hardly believe it . . . I can hardly wait."

"Have you ever considered the possibility that *she* might be a *he?*"

"Nope. Not once. The moment I decided to get pregnant, I put my order in for a girl. The least Steve could do was get that right." His name slipped out unnoticed, but as soon as it left her lips, Carol stiffened. She was doing her utmost to disentangle him from her life, peeling away the threads that were so securely wrapped around her soul. There was no going back now, she realized. She'd confirmed every insulting thing he'd ever accused her of.

The mention of Steve seemed to subdue them both.

"Have you chosen a name for the baby?" Lindy asked a little too brightly in an all too apparent effort to change the subject.

Carol dropped her gaze. She'd originally intended to name the baby Stephanie, after Steve, but she'd since decided against that. There would be enough reminders that Steve was her baby's father without using his name. "Not yet," she answered.

"And you're feeling better?"

"Much." Although she was enjoying staying with Lindy and Rush, Carol longed to go back to her own home. Now that Steve was completely out of her life, living with his sister was flirting with misery. Twice Lindy had tried to casually bring Steve into their conversation. Carol had swiftly stopped her both times, but she didn't know who it was harder on — Lindy or herself. She didn't want to hear about Steve, didn't want to think about him.

Not anymore. Not again.

"So how are you feeling, young lady?" Dr.

Stewart asked as he walked into the examination room. "I'll have you know you gave us all quite a scare."

"That's what I hear." This was her first appointment to see Dr. Stewart since she'd left the hospital. She'd been through a series of visits with the surgeon, Dr. Elgin, and everything was progressing as it should with the post-surgery healing.

"And how's that little fighter been treating you lately?" he asked with an affectionate chuckle, eyeing Carol's tummy. "Is the baby moving regularly now?"

She nodded eagerly. "All the time."

"Excellent."

"She seems determined to make herself felt."

"This is only the beginning," Dr. Stewart said chuckling. "Wait a few months and then tell me what you think."

The nurse came into the room and Carol lay back on the examination table while the doctor listened for the baby's heartbeat. He grinned and Carol smiled back. Her world might be crumbling around the edges, but the baby filled her with purpose and hope for a brighter future.

"You've returned to work?"

She nodded. "Part-time for the next couple of weeks, then full-time depending on how tired I get. Despite everything, I actually feel terrific."

He helped her into an upright position. "It's

little wonder after what you went through — anything is bound to be an improvement." As he spoke he made several notations in her file. "You were one sick young lady. I don't mind telling you," Dr. Stewart added, looking up from her chart, "I was greatly impressed with that young man of yours."

Carol's smile was forced and her heart lurched at the reference to Steve. "Thank you."

"He wouldn't leave your side — not for a moment. Dr. Elgin commented on the fact just the other day. We both believe it was his love that got you through those darkest hours. He was determined that you live." He paused and chuckled softly. "I don't think God Himself would have dared to claim you."

Carol dropped her gaze, not knowing how to comment.

"He's a fine young man. Navy?"

"Yes."

"Give him my regards, will you?"

Carol nodded, her eyes avoiding his.

"Continue with the vitamins and make an appointment to see me in a couple of weeks." He gently patted Carol's hand and moved out of the room.

From the doctor's office, Carol returned to work. But when she pulled into the Boeing parking lot, she sat in her car for several moments, mulling over what Dr. Stewart had told her.

It was Steve's voice that called to her in the

dark fog. Steve had been the one who'd comforted her. And when she'd felt the pull of the night, it was he who had demanded she return to the light. According to Dr. Stewart, he'd refused to leave her side.

Carol hadn't known.

She was stunned. She'd purposely lied to him, wanting to hurt him for being so insensitive about the possibility of the surgery claiming their baby's life. She'd been confused and angry because so much of what he wanted for her revealed his lack of faith in her integrity.

She'd sent him away and yet he'd refused to leave her to suffer through the ordeal alone.

Before she returned to her own job section, Carol stopped off to see Lindy.

"Hi," Lindy greeted, looking up from her desk. "What did the doctor have to say?"

"Take your vitamins and see me in two weeks."

"That sounds profound."

Carol scooted a chair toward Lindy's desk and clasped her purse tightly between her hands. The action produced a wide-eyed stare from her former sister-in-law.

"Something Dr. Stewart did say was profound," Carol stated in even tones, although the information Dr. Stewart had given her had shaken her soul.

"Oh? What?"

"He told me Steve was with me every minute after the surgery. He claimed it was Steve who got me through it alive."

"He was there, all right," Lindy confirmed readily. "No one could get him to leave you. You know how stubborn he is. I think he was afraid that if he walked away, you'd die."

"You didn't tell me that."

"Of course I didn't! If you'll recall, I've been forbidden to even mention his name. You practically have a seizure if I so much as hint that there could be someone named Steve distantly related to either of us."

"But I'd told him the baby wasn't his. . . . I sent him away."

"You told him what?" Lindy demanded, her eyes as round as dinner plates. "Why? Carol, how could you? Oh, good grief — it isn't any wonder you two have problems. It's like watching a boxing match. You seem to take turns throwing punches at each other."

"He . . . didn't say anything?"

"No. Steve never tells me what's going on in his life. No matter what's happened between you two, he won't say a word. I still don't know the reason you divorced in the first place. Even Rush isn't sure what happened. Steve's like that — he keeps everything to himself."

"And he stayed with me, even after I said I wouldn't remarry him," Carol murmured, feeling worse by the moment.

"There will never be anyone else for him but you, Carol," Lindy murmured. Some of the indignation had left her, but she still carried an affronted look, as if she wanted to stand up and defend her brother.

Carol didn't need Lindy's outrage in order to feel guilty. Lying had never set well with her, but Steve had hurt her so badly. She would like to think that she'd been delirious with pain at the time and not herself, but that wasn't the case. When she'd told Steve that she was going to accept another man's marriage proposal, she'd known exactly what she was doing.

"I owe him so much," Carol murmured absentmindedly.

"According to the surgeon and Dr. Stewart, you owe Steve your life."

Carol's gaze held Lindy's. "Why didn't you say something earlier?"

Lindy tossed her hands into the air. "You wouldn't let me. Remember?"

"I know . . . I'm sorry." Carol felt like weeping. Lindy was right, so very right. Her relationship with Steve was like a championship boxing match. Although they loved each other, they continued to strike out in a battle of words and deeds.

It wasn't until after she got home and had time to think matters through that Carol decided what she needed to do — what she had to do.

It wouldn't be easy.

Steve read the directions on the back of the frozen dinner entrée and turned the dial on the oven to the appropriate setting. He never had been much of a cook, choosing to eat most of his meals out. Lately, however, even that was more of an effort than he wanted to make. He'd been reduced to frozen TV dinners.

While they were married, Carol had —

Steve ground his thoughts to a screeching halt as he forced the name of his ex-wife from his mind. It astonished him how easily she slipped in where he desperately didn't want her. Yet he was doing everything he could to try to forget the portion of his life that they'd shared.

But that was more easily said than done.

He hadn't asked Lindy about Carol since she'd been released from the hospital. He wanted to know if Todd Larson was giving her the time she needed from work to heal properly. The amount of control it demanded to avoid the subject of Carol with his sister depleted his energy. He was like a man lost in the middle of a desert, dying of thirst. And water was well within sight, but he dared not drink.

Carol had her own life, and now that she and the baby were safe, she was free to seek her own happiness. As he could — only there would be little contentment in his life without her.

The sound of the doorbell caught him by surprise. He tossed the frozen dinner into the oven and headed to the front door, determined to get rid of whoever was there. He wasn't in any mood for company.

"Hello, Steve."

Carol stood on the other side of the threshold, and he was so shocked to see her that someone could have blown him over with the toot of a toy whistle.

"Carol . . . how are you?" he asked, his voice stiff, his body tense as though mentally preparing for pain.

"I'm doing much better."

She answered him with a gentle smile that spoke of reluctance and regret. Just looking at her tore through his middle.

"Would you like to come in?" he asked. Refusing her entry would be rude, and they'd done more than their share of hurting each other.

"Please."

He stepped aside, pressing himself against the door. She looked well, her coloring once more pink and healthy. Her eyes were soft and appealing when he dared to meet her gaze, which took effort to avoid.

Carol stood in the center of his living room, staring out the window at the panorama of the city. Steve had the impression, though, that she wasn't really looking at the view.

"Would you like something to drink?" he asked when she didn't speak immediately.

"No thanks . . . this will only take a moment."

Now that he'd found his bearings, Steve forced himself to relax.

"I was in to see Dr. Stewart this afternoon," she said, and her voice pitched a little as if she were struggling to get everything out. "He . . . he told me how you were with me after the surgery."

"Listen, Carol, if you've come to thank me, it isn't necessary. If you'd told me who the baby's father is, I would have gone for him. He could have stayed with you, but —"

"I lied," Carol interrupted, squaring her shoulders.

He let her words soak into his mind before he responded. "About what?"

"Marrying the baby's father. I told you that because I was so hurt by what you'd said."

"What I'd said?" He couldn't recall doing or saying anything to anger her. The fact was, he'd done everything possible to show her how much he loved and cared about her.

"You suggested it would be better if I did lose this child," she murmured, and her voice trembled even more, "because next time you could be certain you were the father."

She seemed to want him to respond to that.

"I remember saying something along those lines."

Carol closed her eyes as if her patience was depleted and she was seeking another share. "I couldn't take any more of your insults, Steve."

Everything he said and did was wrong when it came to Carol. He wanted to explain, but doubted that it would do any good. "My concern was for you. Any husband would have felt the same way, pregnancy or no pregnancy."

"You aren't my husband."

"I wanted to be."

"That was another insult!" she cried, and a sheen of tears brightened her eyes.

"My marriage proposal was an insult?" he shouted, hurt and stunned.

"Yes . . . no. The offer to leave the Navy was what bothered me most."

"Then far be it from me to offend you again." There was no understanding this woman. He was willing to give up everything that had ever been important to him for her sake, and she threw the offer back in his face with some ridiculous claim. To hear her tell it, he'd scorned her by asking her to share his life.

The silence stretched interminably. They stood only a few feet apart, but the expanse of the Grand Canyon could have stretched between them for all the communicating they were doing.

The problem, Steve recognized, was that they were both so battle scarred that it was almost impossible for them to talk to each other. Every word they muttered became suspect. No subject was safe. They weren't capable of discussing the weather without finding something to fight about.

"I didn't come here to argue with you," Carol said in weary, reluctant tones. "I wanted to thank you for everything you did. I apologize for lying to you — it was a rotten thing to do."

It was on the tip of his tongue to suggest that he'd gotten accustomed to her lies, but he swallowed the cruel barb. He'd said and done enough to cause her pain in the last couple of years — there was no reason to hurt her more. He would only regret it later. She would look at him with those big blue eyes of hers and he would see all the way to her soul and know the agony he viewed there was of his making. Her look would haunt him for days afterward.

She turned and started to walk away, and Steve knew that if he let her go there would be no turning back. His heart and mind were racing. His heart with dread, his mind with an excuse to keep her. Any excuse.

"Carol —"

Already she was at the front door. "Yes?"

"I . . . have you eaten?"

Her brow creased, as if food was the last thing on her mind. Her gaze was weary as though she couldn't trust him. "Not yet."

"Would you like to go out with me? For dinner?"

She hesitated.

"The last time you were at the apartment, you said something about a restaurant you wanted to try close to here," he said, reminding her. She'd come to his place with a silly button in her hand and lovemaking on her mind. Things had been bad between them then, and had gone steadily downhill ever since.

She nodded. "The Mexican Lindo."

"Shall we?"

Still she didn't look convinced. "Are you sure this is what you want?"

Now it was his turn to nod. He wanted it so much he could have wept. "Yes, I want this," he admitted.

Some of the tiredness left her eyes and a gentle smile touched her lovely face. "I want it, too."

Steve felt like leaping in the air and clicking his heels. "I'll be just a minute," he said hurriedly. He walked into his kitchen and with a quick twist of his wrist, he turned off the oven. He would toss the aluminum meal later.

For now, he had a dinner date with the most beautiful woman in the world.

Chapter Fifteen

Elaborately decorated Mexican hats adorned the white stucco walls of the restaurant. A spicy, tangy scent wafted through the dining area as Carol and Steve read the plastic-coated menu.

Steve made his decision first.

"Cheese enchiladas," Carol guessed, her eyes linking with his.

"Right. What are you going to have?"

She set aside the menu. "The same thing — enchiladas sound good."

The air between them remained strained and awkward, but Carol could sense how desperately they were each trying to ignore it.

"How are you feeling?" Steve asked after a cumbersome moment of silence. His eyes were warm and tender and seemed to caress her every time he looked in her direction.

"A thousand times better."

He nodded. "I'm glad." He lifted the fork and absently ran his fingers down the tines.

"Dr. Stewart asked me to give you his regards," Carol said in an effort to make conversation. There were so few safe topics for them.

"I like him. He's got a lot of common sense."

"The feeling's mutual — Dr. Stewart couldn't say enough good things about you."

Steve chuckled. "You sound surprised."

"No. I know the kind of man you are." Loving, loyal, determined, proud. Stubborn. She hadn't spent five years of her life married to a stranger.

The waitress came to take their order, and returned a couple of minutes later with a glass of milk for Carol and iced tea for Steve.

"I'm pleased we have this opportunity to talk before I'm deployed," he said, and his hand closed around the tall glass.

"When will you be leaving?"

"In a couple of weeks."

Carol nodded. She was nearly six months pregnant now and if Steve was at sea for the usual three, he might not be home when the baby was born. It all depended on when he sailed.

"I used to hate it when you went to sea." The words slipped from her lips without thought. She hadn't meant to make a comment one way or the other about his tour. It was a part of his life and one she had accepted when she agreed to marry him.

"You hated my leaving?" He repeated her words as though he was certain he'd heard her incorrectly. His gaze narrowed. "You used to see me off with the biggest smile this side of the Mississippi. I always thought you were happy to get me out of your hair."

"That was what I wanted you to think," she confessed with some reluctance. "I might have been smiling on the outside, but on the inside I was dreading every minute of the separation."

"You were?"

"Three months may not seem like a long time to you, but my life felt so empty when you were on the *Atlantis*." The first few years of their marriage, Carol had likened Steve's duty to his sub to a deep affection for another woman who whimsically demanded his attention whenever she wanted him. It wasn't until later that she realized how silly it was to be jealous of a nuclear submarine. She'd done everything possible to keep occupied when he was at sea.

"But you took all those community classes," he argued, breaking into her thoughts. "I swear you had something scheduled every night of the week."

"I had to do something to fill the time so I wouldn't go stir crazy."

"You honestly missed me?"

"Oh, Steve, how could you have doubted it?"

He flattened his hands on the table and slowly shook his head. "But I thought . . . I honestly believed you enjoyed it when I was away. You used to tell me it was the only time you could get anything accomplished." His voice remained low and incredulous. "My being underfoot seemed to be a detriment to all your plans."

"You had to know how I felt, or you wouldn't have suggested leaving the Navy."

Steve lowered his gaze and shrugged. "That offer was for me as much as you."

"So you could keep an eye on me — I figured that out on my own. If you held a regular nine-to-five job, then you could keep track of my every move and make sure there wasn't any opportunity for me to meet someone else."

"I imagine you found that insulting."

She nodded. "I don't know any woman who wouldn't."

A heavy silence followed, broken only by the waitress delivering their meals and reminding them that the plates were hot.

Steve studied the steaming food. "I suppose that was what you meant when you said my marriage proposal was an insult?"

Carol nodded, regretting those fiery words now. It wasn't the proposal, but what had followed that she'd taken offense to. "I could have put it a little more tactfully, but generally, yes."

Steve expelled his breath forcefully and reached for his fork. "I can't say I blame you. I guess I wasn't thinking straight. All I knew was that I loved . . . love you," he corrected. "And I wanted us to get married. Leaving the Navy seemed an obvious solution."

Carol let that knowledge soak into her thoughts as she ate. They were both quiet, contemplative, but the silence, for once, wasn't oppressive.

"I dreaded your coming home, too," Carol confessed partway through her meal.

Steve's narrowed gaze locked with hers, and his jaw clenched until she was sure he would damage his teeth, but he made no comment. It took her a moment to identify his anger. He'd misconstrued her comments and assumed the worst — the way he always did with her. He thought she was referring to the guilt she must have experienced upon his return. Hot frustration pooled in the pit of her stomach, but she forced herself to remain calm and explain.

"I could never tell what you were thinking when you returned from a deployment," she whispered, her voice choked and weak. "You never seemed overly pleased to be back."

"You're crazy. I couldn't wait to see you."

"It's true you couldn't get me in bed fast enough, but I meant in other ways."

"What ways?"

She shrugged. "For the first few days and sometimes even longer, it was like you were a different man. You would always be so quiet . . . so detached. There was so little emotion in your voice — or your actions."

"Honey, I'd just spent a good portion of that tour four hundred feet below sea level. We're trained to speak in subdued, monotone voices. If my voice inflections bothered you, why didn't you say something?"

She dropped her gaze and shrugged. "I was so pleased to have you back that I didn't want to say or do anything to cause an argument. It was such a small thing, and I would have felt like a fool for mentioning it."

Steve took a deep breath. "I know what you mean — I couldn't very well comment on how glad you were to see me leave without sounding like an insecure jerk — which I was. But that's neither here nor there."

"I wish I'd said something now, but I was trying so hard to be the kind of wife you wanted. Please know that I was always desperately lonely without you."

Steve took a couple more bites, but his interest in the food had obviously waned. "I can understand why you felt the need for . . . companionship."

Carol froze and a thread of righteous anger weaved it's way down her spine. "I'm going to forget you said that," she murmured, having difficulty controlling her trembling voice.

Steve looked genuinely surprised. "Said what?"

Carol simply shook her head. They would only argue if she pressed the subject, and she didn't have the strength for it. "Never mind."

Her appetite gone, she pushed her plate aside. "You used to sit and stare at the wall."

"I beg your pardon?" Steve was finished with his meal, too, and scooted his plate aside.

"When you came home from a tour," she explained. "For days afterward, you hardly did a thing. You were so detached."

"I was?" Steve mulled over that bit of insight. "Yes, I guess you're right. It always takes me a few days to separate myself from the my duties aboard the *Atlantis*. It's different aboard the sub, Carol. I'm different. When I'm home, especially after being at sea several weeks, it takes time to make the adjustment."

"You're so unfeeling . . . I don't know how to explain it. Nothing I'd say or do would get much reaction from you. If I proudly showed off some project I'd completed in your absence, you'd smile and nod your head or say something like 'That's nice, dear.' "

Steve grinned, but the action revealed little amusement. "Reaction is something stringently avoided aboard the sub, too. I'm an officer. If I panic, everyone panics. We're trained from the time we're cadets to perform our duties no matter what else is happening. There's no room for emotion."

Carol chewed on the corner of her lower lip.

"Can you understand that?"

She nodded. "I wish I'd asked you about all this years ago."

"I didn't realize I behaved any differently. It was always so good to get home to you that I didn't stop to analyze my behavior."

The waitress came and took away their plates.

"We should have been honest with each other instead of trying to be what we thought the other person wanted," Carol commented, feeling chagrined that they'd been married five years and had never really understood each other.

"Yes, we should have," he agreed. "I'm hoping it isn't too late for us to learn. We could start over right now, determined to be open and honest with each other."

"I think we should," Carol agreed, and smiled.

Steve's hand reached across the table for hers. "I'd like us to start over in other ways, too — get to know each other. We could start dating again the way we did in the beginning."

"I think that's a good idea."

"How about walking down to the waterfront for an ice-cream cone?" he suggested after he'd paid the tab.

Carol was stuffed from their dinner, but did not want their evening to end. Their love had been given a second chance, and she was grabbing hold of it with both hands. They were wiser this time, more mature and prepared to proceed cautiously.

"Are you insinuating that I need fattening up?" she teased, lacing her fingers with his.

"Yes," he admitted honestly.

"How can you say that?" she asked with a soft laugh. She may have lost weight with the surgery, but the baby was filling out her tummy nicely, and it was obvious that she was pregnant. "I eat all the time now. I didn't realize how sick I'd been and now everything tastes so good."

"Cherry vanilla?"

"Ooo, that sounds wonderful. Double-decker?"

"Triple," Steve answered and squeezed her hand.

Lacing their fingers like high-school sweethearts, they strolled down to the steep hill toward the waterfront like young lovers eager to explore the world.

As he promised, Steve bought them each huge ice-cream cones. They sat on one of the benches that lined the pier and watched the gulls circle overhead.

Carol took a long, slow lick of the cool dessert and smiled when she noted Steve watching her. "I told you I've really come to appreciate my food lately."

His gaze fell to the rounded swell of her stomach. "What did Dr. Stewart have to say about the baby?"

Carol flattened her hand over her abdomen and glowed with an inner happiness that came to her whenever she thought about her child. "This kid is going to be just fine."

He darted his gaze away as though he was uncomfortable even discussing the pregnancy. "I'm pleased for you both. You'll be a good mother, Carol."

Once more frustration settled on her shoulders like a dark shroud. Steve still didn't believe the baby was his. She wasn't going to argue with him. He was smart enough to figure it out.

"Do you need anything?" he surprised her by asking next. "I'd be happy to do what I can to help. I'm sure the medical expenses wreaked havoc with your budget, and you're probably counting on that income to buy things for the baby. I'd like to pitch in, if you'd let me."

His offer touched her heart and she took a minute to swallow the tears that burned the back of her eyes at his generosity.

"Thank you, Steve, that means a lot to me, but I'm all right financially. It'll be tight for a couple of months, but nothing I can't handle. I've managed to save quite a bit over the past year."

He stood, buried his hands in his pockets and walked along the edge of the pier. Carol joined him, licking the last of the ice cream off her fingertips.

Steve looked down and smiled into her eyes. "Here," he said and used his index finger to wipe away a smudge near the corner of her mouth.

He paused and his gaze seemed to consume her face. His eyes, so dark and compelling, studied her as if she were some angelic being and he was forbidden to do anything more than gaze upon her. His brow compressed and his eyes shifted to her mouth. As if against his will, he ran his thumb along the seam of her lower lip and gasped softly when her tongue traced his handiwork. He tested the slickness with the tip of his finger, slowly sliding it back and forth, creating a delicate kind of friction.

Carol was filled with breathless anticipation. Everything around them, the sights, the sounds, the smells of the waterfront, seemed to dissolve with the feeling. He wanted to kiss her, she could feel it with every beat of her heart. But he held back.

Then, in a voice that was so low, so quiet, it could hardly be counted as sound, he said. "Can I?"

In response, Carol turned and slipped her arm around his neck. His eyes watched her, and a fire seemed to leap from them, a feral glow that excited her all the more.

She could feel the tension in him, his whole body seemed to vibrate with it.

His mouth came down on hers, open and eager. Carol groaned and instinctively swayed closer to him. His tongue plunged quickly and deeply into her mouth and she met it greedily. He tasted and teased and withdrew, then repeated the game until the savage hunger in them both had been pitched to a fevered level. Still his lips played over hers, and once the urgent need had been appeased, the kiss took on a new quality. His mouth played a slow, seductive rhythm over hers — a tune with which they were both achingly familiar.

He couldn't seem to get enough of her and even after the kiss had ended, he continued to take short, sweet samples of her lips, reluctant to part for even a minute. Finally he buried his head in the curve of her neck and took in short raspy breaths.

Carol surfaced in slow, reluctant degrees, her head buzzing. She clung to him as tightly as he held on to her.

"We have an audience," Steve whispered with

no element of alarm apparent in his tone or action.

Carol opened her eyes to find a little girl about five years old staring up at them.

"My mom and dad do that sometimes," she said, her face wrinkled with displeasure, "but not where lots of people can see them."

"I think you have a smart mom and dad," Steve answered, his voice filled with chagrin. Gently he pulled away from Carol and wrapped his arm around her waist, keeping her close to his side. " 'Bye," he told the preschooler.

" 'Bye," she said with a friendly wave, and then ran back to a boy who appeared to be an older brother who was shouting to gain her attention.

The sun was setting, casting a rose-red hue over the green water.

They walked back to where Steve had parked his car and he opened her door for her. "Can I see you again?" he asked, with an endearing shyness.

"Yes."

He looked almost surprised. "How about tomorrow night? We could go to a movie."

"I'd like that. Are you going to buy me popcorn?"

He smiled, and from the look in his eyes he would be willing to buy her the whole theater if he could.

Chapter Sixteen

Steve found himself whistling as he strolled up the walkway to Carol's house. He felt as carefree as a college senior about to graduate. Grand adventures awaited him. He had every detail of their evening planned. He would escort Carol to the movies, as they'd agreed, then afterward he would take her out for something to eat. She needed to gain a few pounds and it made him feel good to spend money on her.

When they arrived back at the house, she would invite him in for coffee and naturally he would agree. Once inside it would take him ten . . . fifteen minutes at the most to steer her into the bedroom. He was starved for her love, famished by his need for her.

The kiss they'd shared the night before had convinced him this was necessary. He was so crazy in love with this woman that he couldn't wait another night to take her to bed. She was right about them starting over — he was willing to do that. It was the going-nice-and-slow part he objected to. He understood exactly what she intended when she decided they could start over. It was waiting for the lovemaking that confused him. Good Lord, they'd been married five years. It wasn't as if they were virgins anticipating their wedding night.

"Hi," Carol said and smiled, opening the door for him.

"Hi." Steve couldn't take his eyes off her. She was wearing the blue maternity dress he'd bought for her the day he'd followed her around like the KGB. "You look beautiful," he said in what had to be the understatement of the year. He'd heard about women having a special glow about them when they were pregnant — Carol had never been more lovely than she was at that moment.

"Do you like it?" she asked and slowly whirled around showing off the dress to full advantage. "Lindy bought it for me. She said she found it on sale and couldn't resist. It was the craziest thing because I'd tried on this very dress and loved it, but decided I really couldn't afford to be spending money on myself. She gave me a silver baby rattle, too. I have a feeling Aunt Lindy is going to spoil this baby."

"You look . . . marvelous."

"I'm getting so fat," she said, and chuckled. To prove her point, she scooped her hands under the soft swell of her abdomen and turned sideways to show him. She smiled, and her eyes sparkled as she jerked her head toward him and announced, "The baby just kicked."

"Can I feel?" Steve had done everything he could to convince himself this child was his. Unfortunately he knew otherwise. But he loved Carol, and he'd love her baby. He would learn to — already he truly cared about her child.

Without this pregnancy there was no way of knowing if they would ever have gotten back together.

"Here." She reached for his hand and placed it over the top of her stomach. "Feel anything?"

He shook his head. "Nothing."

"Naturally she's going to play a game of cat and mouse now."

Steve removed his hand and flexed his fingers. Some of the happiness he'd experienced earlier seeped out of him, replaced with a low-grade despondency. He wanted her baby to be his with a desperation that threatened to destroy him. But he couldn't change the facts.

"I checked the paper and the movie starts at seven," Carol said, interrupting his thoughts.

He glanced at his watch. "We'd better not waste any time then." While Carol opened the entryway closet and removed a light sweater and her purse, Steve noted the two gallons of paint sitting on the floor.

"What are you painting?" he asked.

"The baby's room. I thought I'd tackle that project this weekend. I suddenly realized how much I have to do yet to get ready."

"Do you want any help?" He made a half-hearted offer, and wished almost immediately that he hadn't. It wasn't the painting that dissuaded him. Every time Carol so much as mentioned anything that had to do with the baby, her eyes lit up like the Fourth of July. His reaction was just as automatic, too. He was jealous, and that was the last thing he wanted Carol to know.

She closed the closet door and studied him, searching his eyes. He boldly met her look, although it was difficult, and wasn't disappointed when she shook her head. "No thanks, I've got everything under control."

"You're sure?"

"Very."

There was no fooling Carol. She might as well have read his thoughts, because she knew and her look told him as much.

"I'm trying," he said, striving for honesty. "I really am trying."

"I know," she murmured softly.

They barely spoke on the way to the theater and Carol hardly noticed what was happening with the movie. She'd witnessed that look on Steve's face before when she started talking about the baby. So many subjects were open to them except that one. She didn't know any man more blind than Steve Kyle. If she were to stand up in the middle of the show and shout out that she was having his child, he wouldn't hear her. He'd buried his head so deep in the sand when it came to her pregnancy that his brain was plugged.

Time would teach him, if only she could hold on to her patience until then.

Steve didn't seem to be enjoying the movie any more than she was. He shifted in his seat a couple of times, crossed and uncrossed his legs and munched on his popcorn as if he were chewing bullets.

Carol shifted, too. She was almost six months pregnant and felt eight. The theater seat was uncomfortable and the baby had decided to play baseball, using Carol's ribs for batting practice.

She braced her hands against her rib cage and leaned to one side and then scooted to the other.

"Are you all right?" Steve whispered halfway through the feature film.

Carol nodded. She wanted to explain that the baby was having a field day, exploring and kicking and struggling in the tight confines of her compact world, but she avoided any mention of the pregnancy.

"Do you want some more popcorn?"

Carol shook her head. "No thanks."

Ten minutes passed in which Carol did her utmost to pay attention to the show. She'd missed so much of the plot already that it was difficult to understand what was happening.

Feeling Steve's stare, Carol diverted her attention to him. He was glaring at her abdomen, his eyes wide and curious. "I saw him move," he whispered, his voice filled with awe. "I couldn't believe it. He's so strong."

"She," Carol corrected automatically, smiling. She took his hand and pressed it where she'd last felt the baby kick. He didn't pull away but there was some reluctance in his look.

The baby moved again, and Carol nearly laughed aloud at the astonishment that played over Steve's handsome features.

"My goodness," he whispered. "I had no idea."

"Trust me," she answered, and grinned. "I didn't, either."

Irritated by the way they were disrupting the movie, the woman in the row in front of them turned around to press her finger over her lips. But when she saw Steve's hand on Carol's stomach, she grinned indulgently and whispered, "Never mind."

Steve didn't take his hand away. When the baby punched her fist on the other side of Carol's belly, she slid his hand over there. She loved the slow, lazy grin that curved up the edges of his mouth. The action caused her to smile too. She tucked her hand over his and soon they both went back to watching the action on the screen. But Steve kept his fingers where they were for the rest of the movie, gently caressing the rounded circle of her tummy.

By the time the film was over, Carol's head was resting on Steve's shoulder. Although the surgery had been weeks before, it continued to surprise her how quickly she tired. She'd worked that day and was exhausted. It irritated her that she could be so weak. Steve had mentioned getting something to eat after the movie, but she was having difficulty hiding her yawns from him.

"I think I'd better take you home," he commented once they were outside the theater.

"I'm sorry," she murmured, holding her hand to her mouth in a futile effort to hold in her tiredness. "I'm not used to being out so late two nights running."

Steve slipped his arm around her shoulders. "Me, either."

He steered her toward his car and opened the passenger door for her. Once she was inside, he gently placed a kiss on her cheek.

She nearly fell asleep on the short ride home.

"Do you want to come in for some coffee?" she offered when he pulled up to the curb in front of her house.

"You're sure you're up to this?" he asked, looking doubtful.

"I'm sure."

Carol thought she detected a bounce to his step as he came around to help her out of the car, but she couldn't be sure. Steve Kyle said and did the most unpredictable things at times.

Once inside he took her sweater, and while he was hanging it up for her, she went into the kitchen and got down the coffee from the cupboard. Steve moved behind her and slipped his arms around her waist.

"I don't really want coffee," he whispered and gently caught her earlobe between his teeth.

"You don't?"

"No," he murmured.

His hands explored her stomach in a loving caress and Carol felt herself go weak. "I . . . I wish you'd said something earlier."

"It was a pretense." His mouth blazed a moist trail down the side of her neck.

"Pretense," she repeated in a daze.

As if he were a puppet master directing her actions, Carol turned in his arms and raised her face to his, anticipating his kiss. Her whole body felt as if it were rocking with the force of her heartbeat, anticipating the touch of his mouth over hers.

Steve didn't keep her waiting long. His hands cradled her neck and his lips found hers, exploring them as though he wished to memorize their shape. She parted her mouth in welcome, and his tongue touched hers, then delicately probed deeper in a sweet, unhurried exploration that did incredible things to her. Desire created a churning, boiling pool deep in the center of her body.

His fingers slipped from her nape to tangle with her hair. Again and again, he ran his mouth back and forth over hers, pausing now and again to tease her with a fleck of his tongue against the seam of her lips. "I thought about doing this all day," he confessed.

"Oh, Steve."

His hands searched her back, grasping at the material of her dress as he claimed her mouth in a kiss that threatened to burst them both into searing flames. With a frustrated groan, he drew his arms around her front, searching. His breath came in ragged, thwarted gasps.

Carol could feel the heavy pounding of his heart and she pressed her open mouth to the hollow at the base of his throat, loving the way she could feel his pulse hammer there.

"Damn," he muttered, exasperated. "Where's the opening to this dress?"

It took Carol a moment to understand his question. "There is none."

"What?"

"I slip it on over my head . . . there aren't any buttons."

"No zipper?"

"None."

He muffled a groan against her neck and Carol felt the soft puffs of warm air as he chuckled. "This serves me right," he protested.

"What does?"

He didn't answer her. Instead, he cradled her breasts in his palms, bunching the material of her dress in the process. Slowly he rotated his thumb over her swollen, sensitive nipples until she gasped, first with shock and surprise, then with the sweet sigh of pleasure.

"Is it good, honey?" he asked, then kissed her, teasing her with his tongue until she was ready to collapse in his arms.

"It's very good," she told him when she could manage to speak, although her voice was incredibly low.

"I want you." He took her hand and pressed

it down over his zipper so that she could feel for herself his bulging hardness.

"Oh, Steve." She ran her long fingernails over him.

Exquisitely aroused, he made small hungry sounds and whispered in a voice that shook with desire. "Come on, honey, I want to make love in a bed."

She made a weak sound of protest. "No." It demanded every ounce of fortitude she possessed to murmur the small word.

"No?" he repeated stunned.

"No." There was more conviction in her voice this time. "So many of our discussions end up in the bedroom."

"Carol, dear God, talking was the last thing I had in mind."

"I know what you want," she whispered. "I think we should wait . . . it's too soon."

"Wait," he murmured, dragging in a deep breath. "Wait," he said again. "All right, if that's what you honestly want — then fine, anything you say." Reluctantly he released her. "I'm going to have to get out of here while I still can, though. Walk me to the door, will you?"

Carol escorted him to her front door and his hungry kiss revealed all his pent-up frustration.

"You're sure?" he asked one last time, giving her a round-eyed look that would put a puppy to shame.

"No . . . I'm not the least bit sure," she admitted, and when his eyes widened even more, she laughed aloud at the excitement that flared to life so readily. "I don't like this any better than you do," she told him, "but I honestly think it's necessary. When the time's right we'll know it."

He shut his eyes and nodded. "I was afraid of that."

Chapter Seventeen

Carol woke before seven Saturday morning, determined to get an early start on painting the baby's bedroom. She dressed in a old pair of summer shorts with a wide elastic band and a Seahawk T-shirt that had once been Steve's. A western bandana knotted at the base of her skull covered her blond hair. She looked like something out of the movie *Aliens*, she decided, smiling.

Oh, well, she wouldn't be seeing Steve. She regretted turning down his offer of help now, but it was too late for second thoughts. She hadn't seen him since the night they'd gone to the movies, nor had he phoned. That concerned her a little, but she tried not to let it bother her.

He was probably angry about her not letting him spend the night. Well, for his information, she'd been just as frustrated as he was. She'd honestly wanted him to stay — in fact, she'd tossed and turned in bed for a good hour after he'd left her, mulling over her decision. It may have been the right one, but it didn't take away this ache of loneliness, or ease her own sexual frustration.

For six years the only real communication between them had been on a mattress. It was long past time they started building a solid foundation of love and trust. Those qualities were basic to a lifetime relationship, and they'd both suffered for not cultivating them.

By nine, Carol had the bedroom floor carpeted with a layer of newspapers. The windows were taped and she was prepared to do the cutting in around the corners and ceiling.

She carried the stepladder to the far side of the room and, humming softly, started brushing on the pale pink paint.

"What are you doing on that ladder?"

The voice startled her so much that she nearly toppled from her precarious perch. "Steve Kyle," she cried, violently expelling her breath. "You scared me half out of my mind."

"Sorry," he mumbled, frowning.

"What are you doing here?"

"I . . . I thought you could use some help." He held up a white sack. "Knowing you, you probably forgot to eat breakfast. I brought you something."

Now that she thought about it, Carol realized she hadn't had anything to eat.

"Thanks," she said grinning, grateful to see him. "I'm starved."

Climbing down the stepladder, she set aside the paint and brush and reached for the sack. "Milk," she said taking out a small carton, "and a muffin with egg and cheese." She smiled up at him and brushed her mouth over his cheek. "Thanks."

"Sit," he ordered, turning over a cardboard box as a mock table for her.

"What about you?"

"I had orange juice and coffee on the way over here." Hands on his hips, he surveyed her efforts. "Good grief, woman, you must have been at this for hours."

"Since seven," she said between bites. "It's going to be a scorcher today, and I wanted to get an early start."

He nodded absently, then turned the cap he was wearing around so that the brim pointed toward his back. Next, he picked up the paint-brush and coffee can she'd been using to hold paint. "I don't want you on that ladder, under-stand?"

"Aye, aye, Captain."

He responded to her light sarcasm with a soft chuckle. "Have you missed me?" he asked, turning momentarily to face her.

Carol dropped her gaze and nodded. "I thought you might be angry about the other night when you wanted to stay and —"

"Carol, no," he objected immediately. "I understood and you were right. I couldn't call — I've had twenty-four-hour duty."

Almost immediately Carol's spirits lifted and she placed the wrapper from her breakfast inside the paper sack. "Did you miss *me?*" she asked, loving the way his eyes brightened at her question.

"Come here and I'll show you how much."

Laughing, she shook her head. "No way, fellow. I'd like my baby's bedroom painted before she makes her debut." Carol noted the way Steve's face still tightened at the mention of her pregnancy and some of the happiness she'd experienced by his unexpected visit evaporated. He'd told her he was trying to accept her child and she believed him, but her patience was wearing perilously thin. After all, this child was his, too, and it was time he acknowledged the fact.

Pride drove her chin so high that the back of her neck ached. She reached for another paintbrush, her shoulders stiff with frustration. "I can do this myself, you know."

"I know," he returned.

"It isn't like I'm helpless."

"I know that, too."

Her voice trembled a little. "It isn't like you really want this baby."

An electric silence vibrated between them, arcing and spitting tension. Steve reacted to it first by lowering his brush.

"Carol, I'm sorry. I didn't mean to say or do anything to upset you. My offer to help is sincere — I'd like to do what I can, if you'll let me."

She bit into her lower lip and nodded. "I . . . I was being oversensitive, I guess."

"No," he hurried to correct her, "the problem is mine, but I'm dealing with it the best way I know how. I need time, that's all."

His gaze dropped to her protruding stomach and Carol saw a look of anguish flitter through his eyes, one so fleeting, so transient that for a second she was sure she was mistaken.

"Well," she said, drawing in a deep breath. "Are we going to paint or are we going to sit here and grumble at each other all day?"

"Paint," Steve answered, swiping the air with his brush, as if he were warding off pirates.

Carol smiled, then placed the back of her hand over her forehead and sighed. "My hero," she said teasingly.

By noon the last of the walls were covered and the white trim complete around the window and door.

Carol stepped back to survey their work. "Oh, Steve," she said with an elongated sigh. She slipped her arm around his waist. "It's lovely."

"I sincerely hope you get the girl you want so much, because a boy could take offense at all this pink."

"I am having a girl."

"You're sure?" He cocked his eyebrows with the question, his expression dubious.

"No-o-o, but my odds are fifty-fifty, and I'm choosing to think positive."

His arm tightened around her waist. "You've got paint in your hair," he said, looking down at her.

Wrinkling her nose, she riffled her fingers

through her bangs. Steve's hand stopped her. His eyes lovingly stroked her face as if he meant to study each feature and commit it to memory. His gaze filled with such longing, such adoration that Carol felt as if she were some heavenly creature he'd been forbidden to touch. He raised his hand to her mouth and she stopped breathing for a moment.

His touch was unbelievably delicate as he rubbed the back of his knuckles over her moist lips. He released her and backed away, his breath audible.

Carol lifted her hand to the side of his face and he closed his eyes when the tips of her fingers grazed his cheek.

"Thank you for being here," she whispered. "Thank you for helping."

"I always want to be with you." He placed his hand over hers, intertwining their fingers. Tenderly, almost against his will, he lowered his knuckles to her breast, dragging them across the rigid, sensitive tip. Slowly. Gently. Back and forth. Again and again.

Carol sucked in her breath at the wild sensation that galloped through her blood. Her control was slipping. Fast. She felt weak, as though she would drop to the floor, and yet she didn't let go of his hand, pinning it against her throbbing nipple.

"How does that feel?" he asked, and he rotated his thumb around and around, intensifying the pleasure.

". . . so good," she told him, her voice husky and barely audible.

"It's good for me, too."

His eyes were closed. As Carol watched his face harden with desire she knew her features were equally sharp.

He kissed her then, and the taste of him was so sweet, so incredibly good. His lips teased hers, his tongue probing her mouth, tracing first her upper and then her lower lip in a leisurely exercise. The kiss grew sweeter yet, and deeper.

Steve broke away and pressed his forehead against hers while taking in huge, ragged puffs of air. "There's something you should know."

"What?" She wrapped her hands around his middle, craving the feel of his body against her own.

"The orders for the *Atlantis* came in. I have to leave tomorrow."

Carol went stock-still. "Tomorrow?"

"I'm sorry, honey. I'd do anything I could to get out of this, but I can't."

"I . . . know."

"I got some Family-grams so you can let me know when the baby's born."

Carol remembered completing the short telegramlike messages while they were married. She was allowed to send a handful during the course of a tour, but under strict conditions. She wasn't allowed to use any codes, and she was prohibited from relaying any unpleasant news. She had forty-six words to tell him every-thing that was happening in her life. Forty-six words to tell him when his daughter was born, forty-six words to convince him this baby was his.

His hand slipped inside the waistband of her summer shorts and flattened over the baby. "I'll be waiting to hear."

Carol didn't know what to tell him. The baby could very well be born while he was away. It all depended on his schedule.

"I'd like to be here for you."

"I'll be fine. . . . Both of us will." Carol felt as if she was going to dissolve into tears, her an-guish was so keen. Her hand reached for his face and she traced his eyebrows, the arch of his cheek, his nose and his mouth with fingers that trembled with the strength of her love.

His hands slid behind her and cupped her buttocks, lifting her so that the junction be-tween her thighs was nestled against the strong evidence of his desire.

"I want to make love," she whispered into his mouth, and then kissed him.

He shut his eyes. "Carol, no — you were right, we should wait. We've done this too often before . . . we . . ."

She hooked her left leg around his thigh and felt a surge of triumph at the shudder that went through him.

"Carol . . ."

Before he could think or move, she jerked the

T-shirt off her head and quickly disposed of her bra. Her mouth worked frantically over his, darting her tongue in and out of his mouth, kissing him with a hunger that had been building within her for months. Her fingers worked feverishly at the buttons of his shirt. Once it was unfastened, she pulled his shirttails free of his waistband and bared his chest. Having achieved her objective, she leaned toward him just enough so that her bare breasts grazed his chest.

The low rumbling sound in Steve's throat made her smile. Slowly then, with unhurried ease, she swayed her torso, taking her pleasure by rubbing her distended nipples over the tense muscles of his upper body.

Steve's breathing came in short, rasping gasps as he spoke. "Maybe I was a bit hasty . . ."

Carol locked her hands behind his head. "How long will you be gone?" she asked, knowing full well the answer.

"Three months."

"You were too hasty."

"Does this mean . . . you're willing?"

"I was willing the other night."

"Oh, dear God, Carol, I want you so much."

She rubbed her thigh over his engorged manhood and he groaned. "I know what you want." She kissed him with all the pent-up longings of her heart. "I want you, too. Do you have any idea how much?"

He darted his tongue over one rigid nipple,

feasting and sucking at her until she gave a small cry.

He lifted his head and chuckled. "Good, then the feeling's mutual."

With that, he swung her into his arms and carried her into the bedroom. Very gently he laid her atop the mattress and leaned over her, his upper body pinning her to the bed.

He stared down at her and his eyes darkened, but not with passion. It was something more, an emotion she couldn't readily identify.

"Will I . . . is there any chance I'll hurt the baby?" He whispered the question, his gaze narrowed and filled with concern.

"None."

He sighed his relief. "Oh, Carol, I love you so much."

She closed her eyes and directed his mouth to hers. She loved him, too, and she was about to prove how much.

Carol woke an hour before the alarm was set to ring. Steve slept soundly at her side, cuddling her spoon-fashion, his hand cupping the warm underside of her breast.

They'd spent the lazy afternoon making slow, leisurely love. Then they'd showered, eaten and made love again, with the desperation that comes of knowing it would be three months before they saw each other again.

It was morning. Soon he would be leaving her again. A lump of pain began to unflower inside her. It was always this way when Steve left.

For years she'd hid her sorrow behind a cheerful smile, but she couldn't do that anymore. She couldn't disguise how weak and vulnerable she was without him.

Not again.

When it became impossible to hold back the tears, she silently slipped from the bed, donned her robe and moved into the kitchen. Once there, she put on a pot of coffee just so she'd be doing something.

Steve found her sitting at the table with a large pile of tissues stacked next to her coffee cup. She looked up at him, and sobbed once, and reached for another Kleenex.

"G-g-good m-morning," she blubbered. "D-did you sleep well?"

Obviously bewildered, Steve nodded. "You didn't?"

"I s-slept okay."

Watching her closely, he walked over to the table. "You're crying."

"I know that," she managed between sobs.

"But why?"

If he wasn't smart enough to figure that out then he didn't deserve to know.

"Carol, are you upset because I'm leaving?"

She nodded vigorously. "Bingo — give the man a Kewpie doll."

He knelt down beside her, took her free hand and kissed the back of it. He rubbed his thumb over her knuckles and waited until she swallowed and found her voice.

"I hate it when you have to leave me," she confessed when she could talk. "Every time I think we're getting somewhere you sail off into the sunset."

"I'm coming back."

"Not for three months." She jerked the tissue down both sides of her face. "I always c-cry when you go. You just never see me. This t-time I can't . . . h-hold it in a minute longer."

Steve knelt in front of her and wrapped his arms around her middle. With his head pressed over her breast, one hand rested on top of her rounded stomach.

"I'll be back, Carol."

"I . . . know."

"But this time when I return, it'll be special."

She nodded because speaking had become impossible.

"We'll have a family."

She sucked in her breath and nodded.

"Dammit, Carol, don't you know that I hate leaving you, too?"

She shrugged.

"And worse, every time I go, I regret that we aren't married. Don't you think we should take care of that next time?"

She hiccuped. "Maybe we should."

Chapter Eighteen

"This works out great," Lindy said, standing in line for coffee aboard the ferry *Yakima* as it eased away from the Seattle wharf, heading toward Bremerton. "You can drop me off at Susan's and I can ride home with Rush. I couldn't have planned this any better myself."

"Glad to help," Steve answered, but his thoughts weren't on his sister. Carol continued to dominate his mind. He'd left her only a couple of hours earlier and it felt as if years had passed — years or simply minutes, he couldn't decide which.

She'd stood on the front porch as he walked across the lawn to his car. The morning sunlight had silhouetted her figure against the house. Tears had brightened her eyes and a shaky smile wobbled over her mouth. When he'd opened the car door and looked back, she'd raised a hand in silent farewell and done her best to send him off with a proud smile.

Steve had stood there paralyzed, not wanting to leave her, loving her more than he thought it was possible to care about anyone. His gaze centered on her abdomen and the child she carried and his heart lurched with such pain that he nearly dropped to his knees. There stood Carol, the woman he loved and would always love, and she carried another man's child. The anguish built up inside him like steam ready to explode out of a teakettle. But as quickly as the emotion came, it left him. The baby was Carol's, a part of her, an innocent. This child deserved his love. It shouldn't matter who the father was. If Steve was going to marry Carol — which he fully intended to do — she came as part of a package deal. Carol and the baby. He sucked in his breath, determined to do his best for them both.

Now, hours later, the picture of her standing there on the porch continued to scorch his mind.

"Lindy," he said, as they reached a table, "I need you to do something for me."

"Sure. Anything."

Steve pulled out his checkbook and set it on the table. "I want you to go to the JCPenney store and buy a crib, and a few other things."

"Steve, listen . . ."

"The crib's called the Jenny Lind — at least I think it was." The picture of Carol running her hand over the railing that day he'd followed her came to his mind. "It's white, I remember that much. I don't think you'll have any trouble knowing which one I mean once you see their selection."

"I take it you want the crib for Carol?"

"Of course. And while you're there, pick out a high chair and stroller and whatever else you can find that you think she could use."

"Steve, no."

"No!" He couldn't believe his sister. "Why the hell not?"

"When I agreed to do you a favor, I thought you wanted me to pick up your cleaning or check on the apartment — that sort of thing. If you want to buy things for Carol, I'm refusing you point-blank. I won't have anything to do with it."

"Why?" Lindy and Carol were the best of friends. His sister couldn't have shocked him more if she'd suggested he leap off the ferry.

"Remember the dress?" Lindy asked, and her chest heaved with undisguised resentment. "I felt like a real heel giving her that, and worse, lying about it." Her face bunched into a tight frown. "Carol was as excited as a kid at Christmas over that maternity dress, and I had to tell her I'd seen it on sale and thought of her and how I hoped against hope that it would fit." She paused and glared at him accusingly. "You know I'm not the least bit good at lying. It's a wonder Carol didn't figure it out. And if I didn't feel bad enough about the dress, the rattle really did it."

Steve frowned, too. He'd asked Lindy to make up some story about the dress and the toy so that Carol wouldn't know he'd been following her that afternoon. Those had been dark days for him — and for Carol.

"Did you know," Lindy demanded, cutting into his thoughts and waving her finger under his nose, "Carol got all misty over that silver rattle?" The look she gave Steve accused him of being a coward. "*I* nearly started crying by the time she finished."

Steve's hand cupped the Styrofoam container of coffee. "I'm glad she liked it."

"It was the first thing anyone had given her for the baby, and she was so pleased that she could barely talk." Lindy paused and slowly shook her head. "I felt like the biggest idiot alive to take credit for that."

"If you'll recall, sister dearest, Carol didn't want to have anything to do with me at the time."

Lindy's eyes rounded with outrage. "And little wonder. You are so dense sometimes, Steve Kyle."

Steve ignored his sister's sarcasm and wrote out a check, doubling the amount he'd originally intended. "Buy her a bunch of baby clothes while you're at it . . . and send her a huge bouquet of roses when she's in the hospital, too."

"Steve . . . I don't know."

He refused to argue with her. Instead, he tore off the check, and slipped it across the table.

Lindy took it and studied the amount. She arched her eyebrows and released a soft, low whistle. "I'm not hiding this. I'm going to tell Carol all these gifts are from you. I refuse to lie this time."

"Fine . . . do what you think is best."

Steve watched as she folded the check in half and stuck it inside a huge bag she called her purse.

"Actually you may be sorry you trusted me with this task later," Lindy announced, looking inordinately pleased about something.

She said this with a soft smile, and her eyes sparkled with mischief.

"Why's that?"

Lindy rested her elbows on the tabletop and sighed. "Rush and I are planning to start our family."

The thought of his little sister pregnant did funny things to Steve. She was ten years younger than he was and he'd always thought of her as a baby herself. An equally strange image flittered into this mind — one of his friend Rush holding an infant in his arms. The thought brought a warm smile with it. When it came to the Navy, Rush knew everything there was to know. Every rule, every regulation — he loved military life. Rush was destined to command ships and men. But when it came to babies — why, Rush Callaghan wouldn't know one end from the other. One thing Steve did know about his friend, though — he knew Rush would love his children with the same intensity that he loved Lindy. Any brother and uncle-to-be couldn't ask for anything more.

"Rush will be a good father," Steve murmured, still smiling.

"So will you," Lindy countered.

Blood drained from his heart and brain at his sister's comment. "Yes," Steve admitted, and the word felt as if it had been ripped from his soul. He was going to love Carol's child; he accepted the baby then as surely as he knew the moon circled the earth. When the little one was born, he was going to be as proud and as pleased as if she were his own seed.

"Yes," he repeated, stronger this time, his heart throbbing with a newly discovered joy. "I plan on taking this parenting business seriously."

"Good," Lindy said, and opened her purse once more. She drew out a plastic dish and spoon. "I take it you and Carol are talking to each other now."

Smiling, Steve took a sip of his coffee and nodded, thinking about how well they'd "communicated" the day before. "You could say that," he answered, leaning back in his chair, content in the knowledge that once he returned they would remarry.

"There were times when I was ready to give up on you both," Lindy said, shaking her head. "I don't know anyone more stubborn than you. And Carol's so damn proud; there's no reasoning with her, either."

They'd both learned lessons in those areas. Painful ones.

"Take care of her for me, Lindy," he said, his eyes appealing to his sister. "I'm worried about her. She's so fragile now, delicate in body and spirit."

"I don't think she'll be working much longer, but I'll make a point of stopping in and seeing her as often as I can without being obvious about it."

Her job had been an area they'd both avoided discussing, because ultimately it involved Todd. As much as possible, Steve avoided all thoughts of the sporting good store where Carol was employed.

"I'd appreciate that," he murmured.

"If you think it's necessary, I could suggest picking her up and driving her to work with me."

"That's miles out of your way."

"No, it isn't," she returned, giving him an odd look. "Rush's and my apartment is less than a mile from Carol's place. In fact, I drive right past her street on my way to work anyway. It wouldn't be any trouble to swing by and pick her up."

"True, but Larson's is the opposite direction from the Boeing plant."

"Larson's? What's Larson's?"

"Larson's Sporting Goods where Carol works." Even saying it brought an unreasonable surge of anger. It had always bothered him to think of Carol having anything to do with the store.

"Carol doesn't work at a sporting goods store. She works for Boeing," Lindy informed him crisply, looking at him as though he'd recently landed from Mars. "She's been there over a year now."

"Boeing?" Steve repeated. "She works for Boeing? I . . . I didn't know that."

"Is Larson's the place she used to work?"

Steve nodded, wondering how much his sister knew about Carol's relationship with the owner.

"I think she mentioned it once. As I recall, they were having lots of financial troubles. She was putting in all kinds of extra hours and not getting paid. Not that it mattered, she told me. The couple who owned the place were friends and she was doing what she could to help out. I understand they're still in business. Carol never told me why she decided to change jobs."

Steve chewed on that information. Apparently for all their talk about honest communication they'd done a poor job of it. Again.

Lindy removed the lid from the Tupperware dish and started stirring some orange concoction that faintly resembled mashed carrots.

"Good Lord, that looks awful."

"This?" She pointed the spoon at the container. "Trust me, it's dreadful stuff."

"What is it?"

Lindy's gaze linked with his. "You mean you don't know?"

"If I did, do you think I'd be asking?"

"It's sweet potatoes."

"Sweet potatoes?" he echoed, wrinkling his

nose. "What are you doing eating them at this time of year? I thought they were a holiday food."

"I just told you."

"No, you didn't." He didn't know what kind of guessing game Lindy was playing now, but apparently he'd missed some important clues.

"Rush and I are trying to get me pregnant."

"Congratulations, you already told me that."

"That's why I'm eating the sweet potatoes," Lindy went on to explain in a voice that was slow and clear, as though she were explaining this to a preschooler.

Steve scratched the area behind his left ear. "Obviously I'm missing something here."

"Obviously!"

"Well, don't keep me in suspense. You want to have a baby so you're eating sweet potatoes."

Lindy nodded. "Three times a day. At least, that was what Carol recommended."

"Why would she do that?"

Lindy offered him another one of those looks usually reserved for errant children or unusually dense adults. "Because she told me how well eating this little vegetable worked for her."

Steve's brow folded into a wary frown.

"Apparently she heard this report on the radio about yams raising a woman's estrogen level and she ate them by the bowlful getting ready for Christmas Eve with you." Lindy reached inside her purse and pulled out several index cards. "She was generous enough to copy down some recipes for me. How does sweet potato and ham casserole sound?" she asked, and rolled her eyes. "I don't think I'll be sampling that."

"Sweet potatoes," he repeated.

Lindy's gaze narrowed to thin slits. "That's what I just got done saying."

If she'd slammed a hammer over his head, the effect would have been less dramatic. Steve's heart felt as if it was about to explode. His mind whirled at the speed of a thousand exploding stars. A supernova — his own. Everything made sense then. All the pieces to the bizarre and intricate puzzle slipped neatly into place.

Slowly he rose to his feet, while bracing his hands against the edge of the table. His gaze stretched toward Seattle and the outline of the city as it faded from view.

"Steve?" Lindy asked, concern coating her voice. "Is something wrong?"

He shook his head. "Lindy," he said reaching for her hand and pumping it several times. "Lindy. Oh, Lindy," he cried, his voice trembling with emotion. "I'm about to become a father."

Chapter Nineteen

An overwhelming sense of frustration swamped Steve as the *Atlantis* sailed out of Hood Canal. As he sat at his station, prepared to serve his country for another tour, two key facts were prominent in his mind. The first was that he was soon to become a father and the second, that it would be three interminable months before he could talk to Carol.

He'd been a blind fool. He'd taken a series of circumstantial evidence about Carol's pregnancy and based his assumption solely on a series of events he'd misinterpreted. He remembered so clearly the morning he'd made his less-than-brilliant discovery. He'd gone into Carol's living room and sat there, his heart and mind rebelling at what he'd discovered . . . what he thought he'd learned.

Carol had come to him warm from bed, her eyes filled with love and laughter. He'd barely been able to tolerate the sight of her. He recalled the stunned look she'd given him when he first spoke to her. The shock of his anger had made her head reel back as though he'd slapped her. Then she'd stood before him, her body braced, her shoulders rigid, the proud tilt of her chin unyielding while he'd blasted his accusations at her like fiery balls from a hot cannon.

He'd been so confident. The sweet potatoes were only the beginning. There was the knitting and the milk and a hundred little things she'd said and done that pointed to one thing.

His heart ached at the memory of how she'd swallowed her self-respect and tried to reason with him. Her hand had reached out to him, implored him to listen. The memory of the look in her eyes was like the merciless sting of a whip as he relived that horrible scene.

Dear God, the horrible things he'd said to her.

He hadn't been able to stop taunting her until she'd told him what he wanted to hear. Repeatedly he'd shouted at her to confirm what he believed until she'd finally admitted he was too smart for her.

Steve closed his eyes to the agony that scene produced in his mind. She'd silently stood there until her voice had come in desperate, throat-burning rasps that sounded like sobs. That scene had been shockingly similar to another in which he'd set his mind based on a set of circumstances and refused to believe her.

Steve rubbed a hand wearily across his face. Carol had never had an affair with Todd. She'd tried to tell him, begged him to believe her, and he'd refused.

"Oh, God," he whispered aloud, tormented by the memory. He buried his face in his hands. Carol had endured all that from him and more.

So much more.

Carol was miserable. She had six weeks of this pregnancy left to endure and each day that passed seemed like a year. Next time she decided to have a baby, she was going to plan the event so that she wouldn't spend the hottest days of the summer with her belly under her nose.

She no longer walked — she waddled. Getting in and out of a chair was a major production. Rolling over in bed was like trying to flip hotcakes with a toothpick. By the time she made it from one position to another, she was panting and exhausted.

It was a good thing Steve wasn't around. She was tired and irritable and ugly. So ugly. If he saw her like this he would take one look and be glad they were divorced.

The doorbell chimed and Carol expelled her breath, determined to find a way to come to a standing position from the sofa in a ladylike manner.

"Don't bother to get up," Lindy said, letting herself in the front door. "It's only me."

"Hi," Carol said, doing her best to smile, and failing.

"How do you feel?"

She planted her hands on her beach-ball-size stomach. "Let me put it this way — I have a much greater appreciation of what my mother went through. I can also understand why I'm an only child!"

Lindy giggled and plopped down on the chair. "I can't believe this heat," she said, waving her hand in front of her face.

"*You* can't! I can't see my feet anymore, but I swear my ankles look like tree trunks." She held one out for Lindy's inspection.

"Yup — oak trees!"

"Thanks," Carol groaned. "I needed that."

"I have something that may brighten your day. A preordered surprise."

With an energy Carol envied, Steve's sister leaped out of the chair and held open the front door.

"Okay, boys," she cried. "Follow me."

Two men marched through the house carrying a huge box.

"What's that?" Carol asked, struggling to get out of her chair, forgetting her earlier determination to be a lady about it.

"This is the first part of your surprise," Lindy called from the hallway.

Carol found the trio in the baby's bedroom. The oblong shaped box was propped against the wall. "A Jenny Lind crib," she murmured, reading the writing on the outside of the package. For months, every time she was in the JCPenney store she'd looked at the Jenny Lind crib. It was priced far beyond anything she could afford, but she hadn't seen any harm in dreaming.

"Excuse me," the delivery man said, scooting past Carol.

She hadn't been able to afford a new crib and had borrowed one from a friend, who'd promised to deliver it the following weekend.

"Lindy, I can't allow you to do this," Carol protested, although her voice vibrated with excitement.

"I didn't." She looked past Carol and pointed to the other side of the bedroom. "Go ahead and put the dresser there."

"Dresser!" Carol whirled around to find the same two men carrying in another huge box. "This is way too much."

"This, my dear, is only the beginning," Lindy told her, and her smile was that of a Cheshire cat.

"The beginning?"

One delivery man was back, this time with a mattress and several sacks.

Rush followed on the man's heels, carrying a toolbox in his hand. "Have screwdriver, will travel," he explained, grinning.

"The stroller, high chair and car seat can go over in that corner," Lindy instructed with all the authority of a company foreman.

Carol stood in the middle of the bedroom with her hand pressed over her heart. She was so overcome she couldn't speak.

"Are you surprised?" Lindy asked, once the delivery men had completed their task.

Carol nodded. "This isn't from you?"

"Nope. My darling brother gave me specific instructions on what he wanted me to buy for you — right down to the model and color. Before the *Atlantis* sailed he wrote out a check and listed the items he wanted me to purchase. Rush and I had a heyday in that store."

"Steve had you do this?" Carol pressed her lips tightly together and exhaled slowly through her nose in an effort to hold in the emotion. She missed him so much; each day was worse than the one before. The morning he'd left, she'd cried until her eyes burned. He probably wouldn't be back in time for the baby's birth. But even if he was, it really wouldn't matter because Steve Kyle was such an idiot, he still hadn't figured out this child was his own.

"And while we're on the subject of my dim-witted brother," Lindy said, turning serious, "I think you should know he was the one who bought you the maternity dress and the rattle, too."

"Steve did?"

Lindy nodded. "You two were going through a rough period and he didn't think you'd accept them if you knew he was the one who bought them."

"We're always going through a rough period," Carol reported sadly.

"I wouldn't say that Steve is so dim-witted," Rush broke in, holding up the instructions for assembling the crib. "Otherwise, he'd be the one trying to make sense out of this instead of me."

"Consider this practice, Rush Callaghan,

since you'll be assembling another one in a few months."

The screwdriver hit the floor with a loud clink. "Lindy," Rush breathed in a burst of excitement. "Does this mean what I think it does?"

Steve wrote a journal addressed to Carol every day. It was the only thing that kept him sane. He poured out his heart and begged her forgiveness for being so stupid and so blind. It was his insecurities and doubts that had kept him from realizing the truth. Now that he'd accepted what had always been right before his eyes, he was astonished. No man had ever been so obtuse.

Every time Steve thought about Carol and the baby, which was continually, he would go all soft inside and get weak in the knees. Steve didn't know what his men thought. He wasn't himself. His mood swung from high highs to lower lows and back again. All the training he'd received paid off because he did his job without pause, but his mind was several thousand miles away in Seattle, with Carol and his baby.

His baby.

He repeated that phrase several times each night, letting the sound of it roll around in his mind, comforting him so he could sleep.

Somehow, someway, Steve was going to make this up to Carol. One thing he did know — the minute he was back home, he was grabbing a wedding license and a chaplain. They were getting married.

The last day that Carol was scheduled to work, the girls in the office held a baby shower in her honor. She was astonished by their generosity and humbled by what good friends she had.

Because she couldn't afford anything more than a three-month leave of absence, she was scheduled to return. A temporary had been hired to fill her position and Carol had spent the week training her.

"The shower surprised you, didn't it?" Lindy commented on the way out to the parking lot.

"I don't think I realized I had so many friends."

"This baby is special."

Carol flattened her hands over her abdomen. "Two weeks, Lindy. Can you believe in just two short weeks, I'll be holding my own baby?"

"Steve's due home around that time."

Carol didn't dare to hope that Steve could be with her when her time came. Her feelings on the subject were equally divided. She wanted him, needed him, but she would rather endure labor alone than have Steve with her, believing she was delivering another man's child.

"He'll be here," Lindy said with an unshakable confidence.

Carol bit into her lower lip and shook her head. "No, he won't. Steve Kyle's got the worst timing of any man I've ever known."

Carol let herself into the house and set her purse down. She ambled across the living room and caught a glimpse of herself in the hallway mirror as she walked toward the baby's bedroom. She stopped, astonished at the image that flashed back at her.

She looked as wide as a battleship. Everyone had been so concerned about the weight she lost when she'd been so sick. Well, she'd gained all that back and more. She'd become a walking, breathing Goodyear blimp.

Her hair needed washing and hung in limp blond strands, and her maternity top was spotted with dressing from the salad she'd eaten at lunch. She looked and felt like a slob. And she felt weird. She didn't know how to explain it. Her back ached and her feet throbbed.

Tired, hungry and depressed, she tried to lift her spirits by strolling around the baby's room, gliding her hand over the crib railing and restacking the neatly folded diapers.

According to Lindy and Rush, the *Atlantis* was due into port any day. Carol was so anxious to see Steve. She needed him so much. For the past two years, she'd been trying to convince herself she could live a good life without him. It took days like this one — when the sky had been dark with thunderclouds all afternoon, she'd gained two pounds that she didn't deserve and she felt so . . . so pregnant — to re-

mind her how much she did need her ex-
husband.

The doorbell chimed once, but before Carol
could make it halfway across the living room,
the front door flew open.

"Carol." Steve burst into the room and
slowly dropped his sea bag to the floor when he
saw her. His eyes rounded with shock.

Carol knew she looked dreadful.

"Honey," he said, taking one step toward her.
"I'm home."

"Steve Kyle, how could you do this to me?"
she cried and unceremoniously burst into tears.

Chapter Twenty

Steve was so bewildered by Carol's tears that he stood where he was, not moving, barely thinking, unsure how to proceed. Handling a pregnant woman was not something listed in the Navy operational manual.

"Go away," she bellowed.

"You want me to leave?" he asked, his voice tight and strained with disbelief. This couldn't be happening — he was prepared to fall at her knees, and she was tossing him out on his ear!

With hands held protectively over her face, Carol nodded vigorously.

For three months he'd fantasized about this moment, dreamed of holding her in his arms and kissing her. He'd envisioned placing his hands over her extended belly and begging her and the baby's forgiveness. The last thing he'd ever imagined was that she wouldn't even listen to him. He couldn't let her do it.

Cautiously, as though approaching a lost and frightened kitten, Steve advanced a couple of steps.

Carol must have noticed because she whirled around, refusing to face him.

"I . . . I know the baby's mine," he said softly, hoping to entice her with what he'd learned before sailing.

In response, she gave a strangled cry of rage. "Just go. Get out of my house."

"Carol, please, I love you . . . I love the baby."

That didn't appease her, either. She turned sideways and jerked her index finger toward the door.

"All right, all right." Angry now, he stormed out of the house and slammed the door, but he didn't feel any better for having vented his irritation. Fine. If she wanted to treat him this way, she could do without the man who loved her. Their baby could do without a father!

He made it all the way to his car, which was parked in the driveway. He opened the door on the driver's side and paused, his gaze centered on the house. The frustration nearly drowned him.

Hell, he didn't know what he'd done that was so terrible. Well, he did . . . but he was willing to make it up to her. In fact, he was dying to do just that.

He slammed the car door and headed back to the house, getting as far as the front steps. He stood there a couple of minutes, jerked his hand through his hair hard enough to bruise his scalp, then returned to his car. It was obvious his presence wasn't sought or appreciated.

Not knowing where else to go, Steve drove to Lindy's.

Rush opened the door and Steve burst past him without a word of greeting. If anyone understood Carol it was his sister, and Steve needed to know what he'd done that was so wrong, before he went crazy.

"What the hell's the matter with Carol?" he demanded of Lindy, who was in the kitchen. "I was just there and she kicked me out."

Lindy's gaze sought her husband's, then her eyes widened with a righteousness that was barely contained. "All right, Steve, what did you say to her this time?"

"Terrible things like I loved her and the baby. She wouldn't even look at me. All she could do was cover her face and weep." He started pacing in a kitchen that was much too small to hold three people, one of whom refused to stand still.

"You're sure you didn't say anything to insult her?"

"I'm sure, dammit." He splayed his fingers through his hair, nearly uprooting a handful.

Once more Lindy looked to Rush. "I think I better go over and talk to her."

Rush nodded. "Whatever you think."

Lindy reached for her purse and left the apartment.

"Women," Steve muttered. "I can't understand them."

"Carol's pregnant," Rush responded, as though that explained everything.

"She's been pregnant for nine months, for God's sake. What's so different now?"

Rush shrugged. "Don't ask me." He walked

across the kitchen, opened the fridge and took out a beer, silently offering it to Steve.

Steve shook his head. He wasn't interested in drinking anything. All he wanted was for this situation to be squared away with Carol.

Rush helped himself to a beer and moved into the living room, claiming the recliner. A slow smile spread across his face. "In case you haven't heard, Lindy's pregnant."

Steve stopped pacing long enough to share a grin with his friend. "Congratulations."

"Thanks. I'm surprised you didn't notice."

"Good grief, man, she could only be a few months along."

"Not her," Rush teased. "Me. The guys on the *Mitchell* claim I've got that certain glow about me."

Despite his own troubles, Steve chuckled. He paused, standing in the middle of the room, and checked his watch. "What could be taking Lindy so long? She should have phoned long before now."

Rush studied his own timepiece. "She's only been gone a few minutes. Relax, will you?"

Steve honestly tried. He sat on the edge of the sofa and draped his hands over his bent knees. "I suppose I'm only getting what I deserve." His fingers went through his hair once more. If this continued he would be bald before morning.

The national news came on and Rush commented on a recent senate vote. Hell, Steve didn't even know what his friend was talking about. Didn't care, either.

The phone rang and Steve bounced off the sofa as if the telephone had an electronic device that sent a shot of electricity straight through him.

"Answer that," Rush said, chuckling. "It might be a phone call."

Steve didn't take time to say something sarcastic. "Lindy?" he demanded.

"Oh, hi, Steve. Yes, it's Lindy."

"What's wrong with Carol?"

"Well, for one thing she's having a baby."

"Everyone keeps telling me that. It isn't any deep, dark secret, you know. Of course she's having a baby. My baby!"

"I mean she's having the baby *now*."

"Now?" Steve suddenly felt so weak, he sat back down. "Well, for God's sake she should be at the hospital. Have you phoned the doctor? How far apart are the contractions? What does she plan to do about this?"

"Which question do you want me to answer first?"

"Hell, I don't know." His voice sounded like a rusty door hinge. His knees were shaking, his hands were trembling and he'd never felt so unsure about anything in his life.

"I did phone Dr. Stewart," Lindy went on to say, "if that makes you feel any better."

It did. "What did he say?"

"Not much, but he said Carol could leave

274

for the hospital anytime."

"Okay . . . okay," Steve said, pushing down the panic that threatened to consume him. "But I want to be the one to drive her there. This is my baby — I should have the right."

"Oh, that won't be any problem, but take your time getting here. Carol wants to wash her hair first."

"What?" Steve shouted, bolting to his feet.

"There's no need to scream in my ear, Steven Kyle," Lindy informed him primly.

Steve's breath came in short, uneven rasps. "I'm on my way . . . don't leave without me."

"Don't worry. Now, before you hang up on me, put Rush on the line."

Whatever Lindy said flew out his other ear. Carol was in labor — their baby was going to be born anytime, and she was styling her hair! Steve dropped the phone to the carpet and headed toward the front door.

"What's happening?" Rush asked, standing.

Steve paused. "Lindy's with Carol. Carol's hair is in labor and the baby's getting washed."

"That explains everything," Rush said, and picked up the phone.

By the time Steve arrived at the house, his heart was pounding so violently, his rib cage was in danger of being damaged. He leaped out of the car, left the door open and sprinted toward the house.

"Where is she?" he demanded of Lindy. He'd nearly taken the front door off its hinges, he'd come into the house so fast.

His sister pointed in the direction of the bed-room.

"Carol," he called. He'd repeated her name four more times before he walked into the bed-room. She was sitting on the edge of the mat-tress, her hands resting on her abdomen, taking in slow, even breaths.

Steve fell to his knees in front of her. "Are you all right?"

She gave him a weak smile. "I'm fine. How about you?"

He placed his hands over hers, closed his eyes and expelled his breath. "I think I'm going to be all right now."

Carol brushed a hand over his face, gently caressing his jawline. "I'm sorry about earlier . . . I felt so ugly and I didn't want you to see me until I'd had a chance to clean up."

The frenzy and panic left him and he reached up a hand and hooked it around her neck. Gently he lowered her mouth to his and kissed her in a leisurely exploration. "I love you, Carol Kyle." He released her and lifted her maternity top enough to kiss her swollen stomach. "And I love you, Baby Kyle."

Carol's eyes filled with tears.

"Come on," he said, helping her into an up-right position. "We've got a new life to bring into the world and we're going to do it together."

Sometime around noon the following day,

Carol woke in the hospital to discover Steve sleeping across the room from her, sprawled in the most uncomfortable position imaginable. His head was tossed back, his mouth open. His leg was hooked over the side of the chair and his arms dangled like cooked noodles at his side, the knuckles of his left hand brushing the floor.

"Steve," she whispered, hating to wake him. But if he stayed in that position much longer, he wouldn't be able to move his neck for a week.

Steve jerked himself awake. His leg dropped to the floor with a loud thud. He looked around him as though he couldn't remember where he was or even who he was.

"Hi," Carol said, feeling marvelous.

"Hi." He wiped a hand over his face, then apparently remembered what he was doing in her hospital room. A slow, satisfied smile crept over his features. "Are you feeling all right?"

"I feel fantastic."

He moved to her side and claimed her hand with both of his. "We have a daughter," he said, and his voice was raw with remembered emotion. "I've never seen a more beautiful little girl in my life."

"Stephanie Anne Kyle," she told him. "Stephanie for her father and Anne for my mother."

"Stephanie," Steve repeated slowly, then nodded. "She's incredible. You're incredible."

"You cried," Carol whispered, remembering

277

the tears that had run down the side of Steve's face when Dr. Stewart handed him their daughter.

"I never felt any emotion more powerful in my life," he answered. "I can't even begin to explain it." He raised her hand to his lips and briefly closed his eyes. "You'd worked so hard and so long and then Stephanie was born and squalling like crazy. I'd been so concerned about you that I'd hardly noticed her and then Dr. Stewart wrapped her in a blanket and gave her to me. Carol, the minute I touched her something happened in my heart. I felt so humble, so awed, that I'd been entrusted with this tiny life." He placed his hand over his heart as if it were marked by their daughter's birth and she would notice the change in him. "Stephanie is such a beautiful baby. We'd been up most of the night and you were exhausted. But I felt like I could fly, I was so excited. Poor Rush and Lindy, I think I talked their heads off."

"I was surprised you slept here."

He ran the tips of his fingers over her cheek. "I had to be with you. I kept thinking about everything I'd put you through. I was so wrong, so very wrong about everything, and yet you loved me through it all. I should have known from the first that you were innocent of everything bad I've ever believed. I was such a fool . . . such an idiot. I nearly ruined both our lives."

"It's in the past and forgotten."

"We're getting married." He said it as if he

278

expected an argument.

"I think we should," Carol agreed, "seeing that we have a daughter."

"I never felt unmarried," Steve admitted. "There's only one woman in my life, and that's the way it'll always be."

"We may have divorce papers, but I never stopped being your wife."

The nurse walked into the room, tenderly cradling a soft pink bundle. "Are you ready for your daughter, Mrs. Kyle?"

"Oh, yes." Carol reached for the button that would raise the hospital bed to an upright position. As soon as she was settled, the nurse placed Stephanie Anne Kyle in her mother's arms.

Following the nurse's instructions, Carol bared her breast and gasped softly as Stephanie accepted her mother's nipple and sucked greedily.

"She's more beautiful every time I see her," Steve said, his voice filled with wonder. The rugged lines of his face softened as he gazed down on his daughter. Gently he drew one finger over her velvet-smooth cheek. "But she'll never be as beautiful as her mother is to me right this minute."

Love and joy flooded Carol's soul and she gently kissed the top of her daughter's head.

"We're going to be all right," Steve whispered.

"Yes, we are," Carol agreed. "We're going to be just fine — all three of us."

About the Author

Debbie Macomber, the author of *Thursdays at Eight*, *Between Friends* and the Dakota trilogy, has become a leading voice in women's fiction worldwide. Her work has appeared on every major bestseller list, including the *New York Times*, *USA TODAY* and *Publishers Weekly*. She is a multiple award winner, and there are more than forty-five million copies of her books in print.